FAME WHORE

A Novel By

Mike Hudson

OTHER BOOKS BY MIKE HUDSON

Never Trust The World
Jetsam: Select Writing, 1977-2009
Mob Boss: A Biography In Blood
Diary Of A Punk
Niagara Falls Confidential

For Evita Corby. The most beautiful girl in Hollywood, and the love of my life.

CHAPTER ONE

They were on TV all night. On every channel, it seemed. The witnesses. The innocent bystanders. The survivors. The unwitting stars of whatever reality show dominates the six o'clock news on any given day, trends hard on Google and has 100,000 Facebook likes by noon. There'd been a mass shooting in Hollywood. Twenty-three people were dead including the shooter, who had committed suicide.

For the most part, the victims were hipsters – aspiring actors, models, musicians, writers and artists – drawn to East Hollywood and places like it by an emptiness inside, a hunger for recognition and love unsatisfied by the sorts of familial and romantic entanglements most people settle for in life. For the dead and the wounded and the merely traumatized, for the shooter himself, the killing spree briefly provided the exact sort of venue they'd come to LA to find.

They were all on television.

***

"People were running everywhere, running on top of me, like kicking me, jumping over me. And there were bodies on the ground," an older woman said. *"I froze up. I was scared. I honestly thought I was going to die."*

***

"The image in our heads is stuck in there. I still have my cup right here and honestly, I'm never going to forget this night at all. Because it was the first time I saw something that was real. Like a real-life nightmare that was there, not dreamed of."

"You just smelled smoke and you just kept hearing it, you just heard bam bam bam, non-stop. Shots just kept going, kept going, kept going. I'm with coworkers and we're on the floor praying to God we don't get shot, and the gunshots continue on and on, and when the sound finally stopped, we started to get up and people were just bleeding," a gay guy with a shaved head recounted.

***

"I started seeing flashes and screaming, I just saw blood and people yelling and a quick glimpse of the guy. I was pushed out. There was chaos, we started running," said a young girl with a bad red dye job. She was smoking a cigarette and wearing a pair of Gucci sunglasses. *"Everybody thought it was like fireworks or something like that, and then you just see people dropping and the gunshots are constant. I heard at least twenty to thirty shots within that minute or two. It went on and on and then after we didn't hear anything, we finally got up and there was people bleeding, there was people who obviously might be actually dead or something, and we just ran up out of there. There was chaos everywhere."*

***

"He walked in so casually, like he knew what he was doing. I heard two pops. Everyone was distracted. That was when the panic and the chaos started. He started shooting, and everyone ducked and started screaming. He looked like he was ready to go into battle. It was like he was walking around and having fun. Emotionless," an over the hill rocker wearing a tight black T-shirt told the camera.

***

"There was this girl. She just had this horrible look in her eyes. We made eye contact and I could tell she was not all right. I had to go.

I was going to get shot," said an attractive blonde who'd done some television.

***

Angie slept like a child next to him in the big soft bed. The TV cast the room in a cool blue light. Tom watched the coverage and drank from his coffee cup. With his free hand he rubbed her bare back, the part between the spaghetti straps of the black silk slip she wore to bed every night.

They'd driven by shortly after it happened that morning. The worst mass shooting in California history had gone down six blocks from his apartment.

The newscasters interviewed the cops and the mayor and some hospital officials. They even managed to find someone who *wasn't* there.

"We were getting ready to go, but we couldn't find a babysitter," the hipster housewife said. *"If we had gone, we might be dead. I even got mad at my husband that we couldn't find a babysitter. But I thank God that we're here today to give my daughters big hugs and kisses."*

The screen was filled with images, bodies being wheeled out and weeping victims led by emergency personnel, and Tom was just glad she'd fallen asleep watching "Entertainment Tonight" before the real news came on. Stuff like this always upset her.

Suddenly, a driver's license photo of the man identified as the shooter appeared on the screen and Tom sat bolt upright. Holy shit, he thought. He knew the guy. He'd just seen him yesterday.

"While in the Army, the killer was demoted from sergeant to

specialist and was not granted an honorable discharge when he left the service," a stacked blonde Latina working for *FOX News* said.

She had come to Hollywood hoping to become the next Carmen Electra, but her dreams had been dashed by a somewhat stocky body type – she wore a size four – and she was remanded to covering the LA police blotter for *FOX* local in order to spare herself the humiliation of going back home to San Antonio or Bakersfield or Albuquerque or wherever she came from a loser.

"A military official would not say why the gunman had been stripped of his rank or what negative marks on his record led the Army to disqualify him from an honorable discharge after his six and a half years of service. The official spoke on the condition of anonymity and was not authorized to speak to the media on the matter.

"According to his record, the killer joined the Army shortly after the terrorist attacks of Sept. 11, 2001, and did his initial training at Ft. Sill, Oklahoma. He also was later posted to Ft. Bliss, Texas, Ft. Bragg, North Carolina, Iraq and Afghanistan.

"We're told he initially served as a repairman for the Hawk surface-to-air missile system and eventually trained as a psychological operations specialist. Army psychological operations units, or "psy-ops" units, study ways to trick the enemy in wartime and distribute information that will influence foreign populations.

"Now, despite losing his rank, the shooter's service record shows commendations and medals for achievement, good conduct and 'humanitarian service,'" the woman concluded. *"He also earned a parachutist badge, more commonly called 'jump wings,' for completing the Army Basic Airborne Course at Ft. Benning, Georgia."*

"Jesus Christ," Tom said aloud. He slid out of bed and pulled on a robe and got his cigarettes and lighter from off the nightstand. He walked through the apartment and out onto the back deck. He sat down and smoked, petting the old dog and looking up at the stars in the night sky.

CHAPTER TWO

There is no good. There is no evil. There's only what is, and it means nothing. We are without purpose. At the bottom of it all, everything is just cause and effect, and anything else is a fairy tale. Anyone who thinks they're living a meaningful life is just lying to themselves. There are no plans, no decisions, no choices. No free will, ultimately. There are no deserving poor or undeserving rich. There's just dumb fucking luck.

Harris had believed that. He'd believed it implicitly. And believing it helped elevate him – at the age of 34 – to the position of general manager at the most profitable Jack in the Box restaurant franchise in the entire city of Los Angeles.

It hadn't been easy and, once he'd achieved it, he found it wasn't enough. Because the day finally came when he saw the possibility of something else, something richer and infinitely more exciting. And it ruined him for what he'd been doing, at the same time promising him a world he'd never before dreamed of.

From the minute he woke up, he knew it was going to be a shitty day. His ruthlessness had deserted him. The very qualities that had earned him those three brass and walnut wall plaques as Los Angeles Jack in the Box Manager of the Year seemed petty and useless to him now, not because they hadn't worked but because they had. His felt his headache coming back. He could barely drag himself out of bed.

It finally dawned on him that it didn't matter if you were a manager, or even manager of the year. You worked for Jack in the Box and you were a fucking loser. Like it was tattooed on your forehead. L-O-S-E-R. There was no other way to look at it.

He'd worked for those plaques though, cutting corners everywhere he could. One less slice of tomato or two fewer pickles on any of the 15 different kinds of hamburgers they served, or totally skewing the lettuce, tomato and cheese to chicken pieces ratio in the popular grilled chicken fajita. A fraction of a cent, a thousand times a day, seven days a week.

It all added up.

After all, it wasn't like people who ate at Jack in the Box were picky. They were the kind who drank bacon-flavored milkshakes and gave each other Jack Cash gift cards at Christmastime. The ones whose bad taste and gluttony kept the company afloat even after the deadly e-coli outbreak of '93 killed four children and sickened thousands all across the quad-state area. They didn't notice, they didn't care. They wanted their fucking double cheeseburgers.

And the guys from corporate? Fuck them. They didn't care either. They'd smile and wink. Give him the elbow and a sidelong glance. After all, how do you think they'd gotten to corporate in the first place? They knew perfectly well what he was doing because they'd done the exact same things themselves.

He'd fire team members just before they were to receive their first raise, and would leave team leader spots unfilled to create what he'd read was called "dark time," when whole weekly paychecks could be turned into pure profit. Fuck, the assistant managers didn't do shit anyway, and for the money they were making they could damn well put in some counter time.

The assistant managers. Always looking to take his job, laughing at him behind his back and undermining his authority anywhere they could. He kept his eye on them all the time, humiliating them in front of customers and other employees whenever he had the opportunity. It was too bad Jack in the Box didn't hand out a wall plaque for most assistant managers fired or quit each year, because Harris would've won that one over and over again.

And then there were the internships. Unpaid, of course, and you had to admit that some of those high school *chiquitas* were pretty fucking hot. Mexicans, Salvadorians, some of them could hardly even speak English. But suck the brass off a doorknob? He'd give them the pitch straight out of the manager's handbook.

"Jack in the Box career opportunities aren't just about flipping burgers," he'd tell them. *"They're about chasing dreams, setting goals and frying up your career!"*

He'd run whole shifts with nothing but interns, a team leader and an assistant manager. And bonus points for the experience being bad enough to get the team leader or assistant manager to quit. More dark time and a big part of his success. Yeah, Harris was good all right, the best in all of LA. It said so right on the wall. But it all seemed meaningless to him now. All the scheming and conniving, all the bullshit he took and dished out for a lousy $767.38 a week. He'd wasted his life on trivialities. He didn't even have a girlfriend.

CHAPTER THREE

Tom climbed out of the pool and into the heavy night air pulling on a sweatshirt and walking the few steps over to the glass topped table where he'd left his phone and cigarettes and drink, his lighter and pen and notebook. There was a text message and it was from her.

"i woke up this morning from this empty dream…afraid you were gone…or even worse, that you never existed…please tell me it was only a bad dream…that you love me like no other."

He looked at the time. When it was sent. It was two hours earlier in Los Angeles and she was there now. He wished he was there too, and a chill went up his spine.

He typed with one finger.

"I sat beneath a green awning in the courtyard of the Hotel Caribe, drinking rum and smoking," he wrote. *"It poured buckets and beneath my feet green lichens grew from the red brick pavement. And I thought of you, mi amore, for without you I die… Now the mosquitoes are eating me alive and the bats swoop creepily close…"*

He waited for what seemed to be a long time before she wrote back.

"you might die anyways if you keep living like this…i want to grow old ok? older together with you… don't ever leave me again… please."

Why had he left her? Because he was married to another woman? Because he'd already booked this trip to Mexico and his publisher was picking up the tab? What other stupid reason could he have?

"are you happy…?" she continued. *"i'm not… going out again tonight…need to feel happy again."*

It drove him nuts to think of her going out, having her picture taken with other guys she knew; guys richer and better

9

looking and more famous than he was. Which was a lot of guys in LA. He drank and lit a cigarette.

"*i am not happy...*" he wrote. "*how could i be when i think of you every waking minute? when i dream of you at night?... i feel cut off from my universe. bereft... this place is stunning in its beauty but i would tear it all down for just a glimpse of yours...*

"*everything here, the spanish spoken in the streets, the smell of jasmine, the lush sensuality all around remind me of angelique, far away, who changed everything...*"

He had spent the day looking at apartments for them in the old Colonial district. Italianate manses two hundred years old with airy upper floor balconies of wrought iron reached through French doors overlooking the plaza. Two bedrooms, renting at fourteen hundred pesos a month. They could live there forever, he thought.

"*you are not alone my love...*" she wrote. "*my voice my smell and the lips you long for are there...inside you...*"

Tom didn't tell her about looking at the apartments and he didn't tell her about afterward, when he took Communion at the ancient cathedral for the first time in thirty years. He'd come back to the hotel and became violently ill.

"*Rotten night,*" he wrote instead, not telling her about the screaming knock down telephone drag out he'd had with his wife Rachel, either.

"*why?... maybe because i wasn't there? don't torture yourself baby... save that for me... this is not going to be easy for any of us...*"

She didn't go out that night. They stayed at it, writing back and forth like that, until the sun came up over the old limestone wall of the fort and he went in and went to bed. He'd finished his book and would send the manuscript to New York in the morning on his way out of town.

***

10

The road to the airport seemed familiar and it took a minute for him to realize it was not dissimilar to La Brea Avenue, which was a road you could take to get from Hollywood to LAX, if you were in Los Angeles.

He was not in Los Angeles, however.

He was hungover that morning as he boarded the eight o'clock flight for Mexico City. The Aero Mexico stewardesses wore jaunty red caps with short, belted blue dresses and four-inch stiletto heels and once again Tom remembered why he liked being away from the United States.

All the flying and gunfire and crisp night swims in heavily chlorinated Third World hotel pools over the past month had left him nearly deaf, and as the stewardess gave the safety instructions she looked to him like a tiny tanned doll moving her mouth but making no sound. He imagined she was telling him how much she loved him.

It was November 2, Dia los Muertes, and he thought of Lowry's book and of Markson, who had written so well about Lowry and was dead now himself. It was a short flight – Merida, on the Yucatan peninsula, up to Mexico City. He had no business in Mexico City but to catch a connecting flight to Vegas, north of the border, which was the only place in the world he wanted to be.

Markson had been his great friend and champion, connecting him to the New York literary scene, as it had been forty and fifty years earlier. They'd shared a love of Mexico and of baseball and for beautiful, interesting women.

They'd agreed that it was better to have written than it was to actually be writing and that watching Mexican League baseball with a beautiful, interesting woman so awed by your scary talent she wouldn't bitch because you took her to a goddamn baseball game in Reynosa or Vera Cruz was the best of all.

The stewardess handed him a packet of Florentines, small

cookies filled with a cherry jam, and a cup of black coffee. He looked down on the snowcapped mountains outside of Mexico City.

Vegas was just that much closer to Los Angeles, where he'd left her, and he thought about that. He hadn't wanted to leave, but there was nothing he or anybody else could do about it. The time between then and now had been one long mistake and now his whole life was up for grabs.

Later he sat in the airport bar sipping a mojito. He took out the black covered notebook he kept and read over his impressions of the Yucatan, where there was no war or, really, unpleasantness of any kind. He'd spent eight days there copy editing the book and had been hoping for some kind of action – live shooting or at least some beheadings – so he could sell an article or some photos, as his traveling capital was running low.

But there'd been nothing. No soldiers on the streets even, just regular beat cops. No nervousness in the cafes, no tension in the air and the only thing anyone tried to sell him in the plaza was a Panama hat.

So he edited his book and he swam in the pool, spending the afternoons in one or another of the cafes that lined the streets. He had dinner at the hotel restaurant and went to bed early. Aside from the women, one in New York and the other in LA, there was nothing in the notebook that was even remotely interesting, even to him.

When he finished reading, he took out his pen. He wanted to write again of Angie, for Angie, but it was all too complicated to begin in an airport bar and the best he could come up with was a fragment from another airport layover, a couple of weeks earlier.

"I was in Philly for Joe Frazier's funeral," he wrote. *"I didn't go, of course, but there was no place to be that day but Philly."*

It was the usual stuff. Duller than dishwater and ultimately unsatisfying, but at least he could say he had written, and writing was the thing he did to justify all of the other things he did.

***

Her eyes were green as the color of a Heineken beer bottle, and he wanted to drink every bit of it. They reminded him of all the money she'd finagled from a long line of suckers going back to Hollywood High, where she'd come from, all those years ago. She'd broken hearts from LA to Paris, and all the artists and actors and musicians she left in her wake could have formed some sad club, a legion of losers, like Alcoholics Anonymous, but with her instead of the booze.

He knew all that and he came anyway. She called and he came. She'd had it with the artists and actors and musicians and she called and he came knowing she had the potential to be more dangerous than anything he'd known in Brooklyn or Belfast or Mexico City.

She was a glamour girl all right, a transcendental signifier with a thousand photographs in magazines and on the internet to prove it. High maintenance for sure, but he'd been around long enough to know they all were, all the ones worth having, the ones born pretty and smart and hip in places like New York and LA, the ones who figured out for themselves how to make their own money whether their parents were rich or poor and regardless of whoever it was they happened to take for their first or third husbands.

In the past six weeks he'd been in and out of LA twice, then New York and the jungle of the northern Yucatan and now Vegas.

His wife Rachel waited for him as she always did in the apartment they'd shared for fifteen years on West Forty Seventh Street in Manhattan. She would cry again when he told her he was leaving her; she would hate him even though she loved

13

him. The last time he'd been home, between LA and Mexico, seemed unreal to him, an odd stopover in a life now lived on the road. Although he hadn't realized it then, that was when it was over. That moment. He looked at her and he looked around and he said to himself, "This isn't me. This isn't where I belong."

He'd met Angie a few weeks earlier on the set of a short film shot on some makeshift soundstage out by the airport when he was in LA the last time. He'd written some additional dialogue and she'd played a small role as some kind of jet-setting call girl, and they went out a few times for dinner or coffee while he was there.

Nothing happened. It seemed impossible. Aside from the fact that they lived 3,000 miles away from each other, he was married. Very. They got to know each other, flirted, each thinking it would end once he went back home.

But it didn't end, did it? She enchanted him. He was fascinated by her, not simply because of her stunning good looks but because, despite them – and the fact that men fawned over her and women appeared eager to serve and please her – every time he saw her, Angie seemed to Tom like the loneliest person in the room.

So when he got home he couldn't get her out of his head, and he called her and kept calling her. After awhile, she started calling him back.

He told her he had to see her again and she said he should come back out to LA but there were a lot of reasons he didn't want to do that so he told her he'd meet her in Vegas and finally she said yes.

Now he saw her from across the casino floor. A real hot ticket sitting in a brown leather club chair waiting for him at a low table in one of the lounges, eating from a white tin box of Wintergreen Altoids and drinking cranberry with a twist of lime. She was gorgeous, her tiny fine features and porcelain skin offset by a wild mane of raven hair and impeccably tailored black and grey clothes and he just stood there for a minute taking her in.

Angie hated people and their meaningless little lives. All around her the losers wasted their own time deliberately, filling it with endless chatter and trips to the mall, all the while anesthetizing themselves with anti-depressants, mood elevators or booze and talking to barmaids as though they were friends or to doctors paid to listen to their stupid problems.

"They don't even show up for life," she said with contempt.

The people who willingly gave their power to other people, women to men, poor to rich; failing to realize that – ultimately – it was all up to them and that, really, they could do whatever the fuck they wanted just annoyed her. They didn't know how to dress or eat or even what kind of fucking haircut looked best on them.

She was like a dream to him. A force of nature like the wind. Like the sun in the sky.

He had no idea how to act. He thought of an acquaintance in New York who'd once married a woman for no other reason than he was too cheap or too broke to hire a nanny to look after his children. Ultimately guiltless despite an overwhelming guilt. Beyond guilt, even.

He was doing it again. Throwing the sticks up into the air just to see where they landed. He'd done it with cities and he'd done it with wives. Now he was in Vegas, where all around him the nickel and dimers contented themselves risking nothing but money, calling themselves high rollers and acting as though what they were doing actually constituted gambling.

Soon he would be living three thousand miles away from New York and the only time he would see snow would be on a picture postcard.

"*We are going to be the most hated couple from New York to LA,*" she'd written, knowing he'd leave his wife, toss everything out the window, like any guy would at her siren's call. People would talk.

Tom thought about these things and other things as well, standing on the carpeted casino floor, wearing a copper-colored sharkskin jacket he'd bought at some vintage men's store she'd taken him to on Hollywood Boulevard.

He crossed the room and walked up behind her.

"Hey baby. You wanna fuck?" he said.

It turned out she did. She stood up and kissed him deeply then threw her legs up around his hips and he cradled her ass in his hands. Her arms wrapped around the back of his neck and their tongues pushing and shoving between one mouth and the other like it was some kind of sordid athletic event. He ordered the whiskey to go and on the elevator up to the room she played with his cock through his jeans and he ran his hand up under her blouse to those sweet bare breasts beneath the sheer black cloth. He pushed her against the wall and they kissed and clawed and bit like animals in heat. "Tell me you love me. Say you love me," she said, digging her fingernails into the small of his back.

"I love you baby," he said. "I love you more than anything in the fucking world."

"How much?"

"I love you more than the world. I love you more than God."

She could have asked him to kill somebody and he would have done it. The whiskey sloshed from the rim of the glass to the floor and he took a gulp so as not to waste any more. The elevator doors opened and they spilled out into the hallway to their room and she fell back on the bed, stripping off her clothes on the way down.

Inside she was soft and wet and hot and all he wanted was to be up and in there and instead of two people they were one, like an earthquake or wildfire or some other spontaneous

16

natural disaster. She tore at his forearms with her nails and he felt the sharp pain but it wasn't until a few minutes had passed that he noticed the blood, running down his wrists and hands and smearing onto the thousand thread count Egyptian cotton pillow cases and sheets and the down comforter. He pinned her to the bed and drove deeper and deeper and his sweat mixed with the blood stinging and she moaned and sighed and he felt as though he was drowning.

She knew exactly what to do, what he liked, and she was good at it. The best he ever had.

"Come in me baby," she said. "I want you to come inside me," and she put her hands down there and a moment later he exploded with such intensity that, for a second, he didn't even know he existed any more.

It was winter, and outside the cold desert sun shined bright on the streets and the palm trees and the low dark mountains. The room became an abstraction to him. The drapes drawn black and her eyes and her mouth and her breasts and her pussy and the rage he'd kept inside for all those years. They fucked and fucked and when they were spent and worn and empty he rubbed her back until she fell asleep. He laid next to her touching, intoxicated by the scent of her hair and her sweet sleepy breath.

It was like that for the next five days. Their phones would ring, and sometimes they would answer them. The only light was that from the muted television set. His tongue became familiar with every inch of her body. Once or twice every twenty four hours they would go down to the casino. Wander into one of the restaurants and eat a little. She liked the buffet. He didn't even bother putting his boots on.

***

On the final day they sat across a small table in an airport bar, about twenty minutes before he had to board his flight for New York and forty-five minutes before her flight back to Los Angeles. Her eyes, beautiful beyond all reason, welled with tears.

"Stop it," he told her. He said it abruptly, in the toughest voice he could muster. He didn't want to see it because he felt as though he might choke up himself.

She said she didn't want him to go home and he told her he was home. That wherever she was, that was his home. In the back of a taxicab driving down Tropicana or there at the airport bar. In California or Nevada or Mexico or anywhere she wanted. She loved him even more when he told her that.

"You should marry me," she said to him then. "I deserve you."

***

As the plane taxied down the runway he looked out past the city to the mountains. He wished he had it to do over again, but he always wished that, no matter what it was. He resigned himself to missing her, to the fact that in seven hours he'd be back in New York for who knew how long, and it would be cold and angry and full of hurt.

Why did life have to be like it was? Why did his happiness so often cause another person pain? Another person he cared so deeply about. He was fifty years old and had seen a lot of things but he still didn't know. He only knew that it did and he wished it could be otherwise.

While he thought those thoughts, and his plane left the ground, he looked down on the orange tiled roofs of all the ugly houses in all the shitty subdivisions that make up greater Las Vegas. Angie was still in the airport, being strip searched by a couple of matrons after having made some smart ass remark to a uniformed TSA officer while going through security.

CHAPTER FOUR

Harris had become a Starbucks regular a few weeks earlier, going in there one night for no other reason than Cookie, a high school senior he was banging while she was doing an internship, wanted to go. He'd heard of Starbucks of course, and seen the stores, but had never been. What the hell, he thought.

The coffee was as bad as he'd ever tasted. Like it was burned or something. Worse than Jack in the Box coffee, even. But the people there – sitting on wooden chairs at tables like you see at Ikea and working on their laptops or reading hardcover books – they seemed sophisticated, not like Jack in the Box customers at all.

The guys all looked like they were rock and rollers, though some were probably writers or actors or artists, Harris figured, kind of shifty, making deals on their iPhones, checking their email or updating their Facebook profiles as though they didn't have a care in the world. The women, totally sexed up in skinny black tights and oversize sunglasses with wild red, black or blonde hair. They could have been models or actresses or stars on some TV reality show. Like *professional* beautiful women. His head spun. It was a revelation to him. He was blown away.

The people who worked the counter weren't dumbass high school kids, either; some of them were as old as he was. He found out they were called *baristas* rather than losers, which was what everybody called the people who worked at Jack in the Box.

Despite his tough guy demeanor, Harris possessed a certain childlike naivety that never served him well. It didn't occur to him, for example, that the Starbucks patrons he saw that night might merely have been affecting the look of rock musicians or fashion models or other celebrities. He didn't realize they really made their livings working at one or another of the countless low rent boutiques, record stores and forlorn vegan restaurants begging for attention on Sunset; or that they labored as bartenders or second hand store clerks or bicycle messengers.

For Harris, this strange, newly discovered reality – not simply a place, but the possibility of a whole new way of life -- blinded him to the likelihood that he might just be standing in in the middle of a roomful of poseurs, fake suburbanite hipsters from Tempe or Salt Lake City who lived in Silver Lake now because somebody told them it was "edgy."

Here was something real at last, he thought, and he could be a part of it. An integral part. For the first time, he saw LA as it really was, not just a place with nice weather and pretty girls, not just a town to live in so he wouldn't have to go back to where he was from. He was already scheming.

It was the Starbucks at Hollywood and Vermont and that first night he found himself standing in line behind an incredibly gorgeous woman who took his breath away. Her perfume filled his head and he leaned in close. A shock of long, tangled black hair and china white skin and the big sunglasses that hid her beautiful green eyes beguiled him. The crushed red velvet of her embroidered jacket. She shifted her weight from one black suede boot to the other, lifting one toe and pirouetting slightly on the spike heel. She couldn't have weighed more than a hundred pounds.

She wore her elegance as though she'd been born into it, as if it came to her as naturally as obesity or a genetic predisposition toward cancer might come to another.

It made him feel hipper just to stand behind her in line, and he smiled. He discovered her real power and fell victim to it. Because without saying a word or even looking in their direction, she had the ability to make every man who saw her believe they had a chance with her, that her body and her mind

20

and her soul could be theirs. For her part, Angie had no idea of the effect she had on men, the way conversations stopped when she walked into a room or what they thought about when they went home.

What was a goddess like this doing out on the town alone, he wondered. Fighting the urge to reach out and touch her hair, to lean in and nuzzle the nape of her neck. Cookie the intern chattered on in her stupid seventeen-year-old way about the stupid Will Ferrell movie they'd just seen and what kind of drink she wanted him to order for her once they'd reached the counter. Harris didn't hear a word she said.

What he heard, delivered in the throaty voice of a fallen angel, was the woman's order.

"I'll have a Chai latte soy -- seven pumps, no water, no sweetener. I want it extra hot and I want it extra foamy. I want so much extra foam you have to put it in a separate cup," she said. "Do you think you can do that for me, sweetheart?"

The barista, a man around Harris's own age who wore a diamond stud in his earlobe and had part of a spider tattoo visible on the back of his neck, smiled brightly.

"Will there be anything else, Miss?" he asked hopefully.

"Are those blueberry scones fresh?" she replied.

"Just this afternoon," he said, and she nodded her head, handing him her Platinum American Express card.

"Oh, and I need a venti dark roast as well please," she said.

"Name?" the barista asked, magic marker in one hand and her cup in the other. She let out an annoyed sigh.

"Angie," she said. "The other person knows my name."

Angie, Harris thought. Just like Angelina Jolie.

The guy gave her the blueberry scone and the regular coffee and Harris watched as she walked outside to the patio and a table under the lights where a guy was sitting.

The guy was older and wore a black suit jacket and jeans, but the most noticeable thing about him was that he had some kind of black mutt Chihuahua sitting on his lap. What a fag, Harris thought.

He narrowed his eyes as Angie approached the table and set the paper cup of coffee and the blueberry scone down in front of the guy, then bent at the waist and put her arms around his neck and kissed him, a long and lingering kiss that gave him time to run his hand up the back of her thigh.

When they were through kissing, Angie stood up and Tom reached into the paper bag and pulled out a bit of the scone, which he fed to the Chihuahua, whose name was Rowena. He'd be leaving LA in the morning, having dragged his rewrite out an extra five days, and going home to New York where his wife Rachel was waiting for him.

"There you go, my big girl," Tom said to the dog.

"You're such a good daddy," Angie told him, heading back in to get her own order.

Tom watched her and thought about how she looked almost as good walking away as she did walking toward him. Everything about her flawless. The Ferragamo perfume was intoxicating on her. Her carefully tangled black hair and pale porcelain skin, the big Dolce & Gabanna sunglasses that hid those beautiful emerald eyes and the embroidered Anna Sui jacket. The vintage Chanel boots that pushed up that perfect little ass. The most beautiful girl in Hollywood, he thought.

They'd had fun together. He didn't want to think he was in love with her. He didn't want to think that at all.

Still, he couldn't help but think about how strained things had been with Rachel for most of the past year – she drank more than he did now and he didn't know why – and he wished for an excuse to stay on in Los Angeles. But he'd run out of excuses and the filmmakers had run out of patience and probably money as well. He wondered if he'd ever see Angie again.

The night was beautiful and warm. He petted Rowena and took a sip of the hot coffee. He'd been in LA for nearly a month off and on and was just starting to get his bearings, the points of the compass and the stars in the sky. Back East it was the Big Dipper, but out there is was all about Orion and his belt.

Suddenly, inside the store, Harris felt someone pulling on his jacket sleeve as if waking him from a dream. He felt confused, disoriented.

"What's wrong with you?" he heard Cookie saying.

"Huh?" he stammered. "Wha…?"

He looked back and saw the barista, his diamond stud and spider tattoo, glaring at him with contempt.

"What'll you have, dog?" the guy said again.

But before he could answer, all hell broke loose down the counter.

"ARE YOU FUCKING KIDDING ME?" Angie exploded, holding her cup in one hand and the plastic lid in the other. The baristas moved quickly down to the end of the counter where she stood.

"Are you the manager?" she demanded. Everybody in the place was looking at her. She was brilliant, fierce, fearless and savage, a gorgeous tiny creature, heated and beautiful.

It turned out they'd used regular milk instead of soy and there wasn't enough foam or something. But it didn't matter.

"This never happens at the Starbucks on Los Feliz," she snarled. "No, it's never been a problem."

The manager was apologizing profusely. She said she hoped he didn't like his job because once she got done talking to corporate he was going to lose it. He took the charge off her credit card while Harris watched transfixed. She was fiery, captivating, thrilling. He knew right then and there that this was the kind of woman he wanted, the sort of world he wanted to live in.

But what chance would he have with a woman like that? He smelled like a fucking hamburger. All those years of changing the grease out of the deep fryers, the spoiled produce taken out to the dumpster a thousand times, the pants and shirts so stained with special sauce and ketchup that the water in the washing machine took on an orange hue.

He drove Cookie to the apartment building in the Valley, where she lived with her parents, not saying a word the whole way. He felt a headache coming on. He parked on the street in front of her house and kissed her perfunctorily before pushing her head down to his lap. She could give him a blowjob, that would help him relax, but he'd already made up his mind. First thing in the morning, he'd fire her.

There was nothing Harris could do about it. He couldn't get Starbucks, or Angie, out of his head. On the drive home, he sang an old marching song he'd learned in the Army.

Oh a little bird, with a yellow bill
Landed on, my windowsill.
I lured him in, with a crust of bread.
And then I smashed his fuckin' head.

Harris sang it over and over out loud, from Vermont to Los Feliz and then down Brand to Colorado in Glendale, where his apartment was.

CHAPTER FIVE

It had to happen sooner or later. He was that kind of guy. It's a cliché that Hollywood ruins writers, but what the fuck. He was pretty much ruined already. The challenge in Los Angeles wouldn't be to find somebody else who'd written five books, it would be to find someone who'd read five books, Tom thought laughing.

Because now it was a done deal. Vegas had changed everything.

This wasn't some infatuation, some fling he could have and walk away.

He hadn't planned on it, he didn't mean for it to happen. But it happened, and once it did he couldn't think of anything else. Her faultless beauty consumed him.

After Vegas his world was empty without her. It meant nothing. He knew it the minute he got back to New York, and he knew it throughout the miserable ten days he'd been able to stay there. Rachel was a stranger to him now. He never thought of that apartment as small but suddenly it seemed there was no way for them to avoid each other, even for a few minutes.

When he first got back, he wasn't sure how it would go. He tried to make the best of it. Not Rachel though. She knew exactly how it would go. It was already gone.

"How's my love?" he asked early the next morning as she came into the kitchen for coffee.

"Why don't you fucking call her and find out?" she said, pouring her own and topping it off with a shot of Johnnie Walker Black.

She had been by turns sad and angry, unbearably sad and unspeakably angry, hating and already missing him one after the other. She made no effort to hide her feelings, no attempt to make him feel he was anything other than the piece of shit he was.

She knew him all right. She hadn't stayed with him for all those years and not learned something. He was a liar. You couldn't believe a word he said. He'd lie about what he had for breakfast.

Now he'd gone to fucking California and met a girl. A witch. A rich witch bitch. The one she always knew he'd meet, the one that had made her miserable almost from the day she'd met him herself.

It wasn't fair. When Rachel found him he was finished, drinking and drugging himself to death in some East Village dive, not writing, crashing on some musician friend's couch, essentially homeless after his second wife threw him out on the street. With her advanced degrees from NYU and Duke, her Manhattan social circle and that hip little apartment she had on Avenue A then, Rachel had helped Tom immeasurably, advancing his career and returning him to some semblance of health. And now this. He was leaving her for some botoxed Hollywood fame whore who wouldn't have given him the time of day back then. It wasn't fucking fair.

Finally, she wasn't talking and he wasn't talking and there they were. They'd been together for all those years and now it was over and there was nothing either of them could do about it.

Late at night, Angie would call. She loved him madlessly. She missed him terribly, she would say, and then begin to cry. She couldn't stand to live another day without him. She needed him so bad she was miserable.

"I just checked my emails," she told him. "Things like, 'What's up with you and Tom?' and 'You do know he is married, an alcoholic?' I'm starting to feel like Liz in *BUtterfield 8*."

He laughed.

"I can't wait for our crazy adventure to begin baby," she said. "Lots of fun and fucking ... fucking fun."

"You're the best thing that ever happened to me, Angie. If I didn't give this my best shot, I'd hate myself for the rest of my stupid fucking life," he told her.

He heard a crash from Rachel's bedroom and got up and closed the door to the study. He sat back down at the desk and poured a glass of Glenlivet.

"What was that?" Angie asked.

"Nothing," he said and drank. "Insane day here. Really insane. It's all gonna blow up pretty soon. I'll deal with it."

"I think she wants to hurt you and get revenge. She's like a woman scorned," she said. "I tried to warn you. You should've listened."

"It was stupid trying to be honest and pretending we're all adults," he said. "I should have known better."

"What are you going to do? This is so sad..."

It got so finally he couldn't take it. He'd listen to Rachel cry all day in New York and then to Angie cry all night on the phone from LA. He wanted to do the right thing but there was no right thing. He wasn't getting any sleep. He was too busy making women miserable on both coasts.

You are such a fucking asshole, he thought to himself.

Rachel always drank, but it started getting bad around the time Tom was diagnosed with advanced cirrhosis a few years earlier. Now she drank more than he did, frightened beyond measure at the prospect and certainty of his premature death, and he was the last person in the world equipped to deal with the drama of another alcoholic.

New York was the beginning and LA was the end and all the country in between was just geography, Tom thought, the space and time involved in getting from one to the other. He arranged to have some clothes and a few books and other things shipped to Angie's Los Feliz address and bought a plane ticket online. He took Rachel to the bank and they split everything they had down the middle. It didn't take long.

Rachel cried a little and they went to lunch.

***

"Hi. Did anyone turn in a pair of sunglasses?"

He'd gotten all the way to the gate before noticing they were missing and running back. The lady from Homeland Security gave him the once over.

"What'd they look like?" she asked.

"Like Ray Bans," he said.

She picked up his glasses and examined them.

"It doesn't say Ray Ban," she said.

"I didn't say they were Ray Bans. You asked me what they looked like and I said they looked like Ray Bans. They say 'Made in China' on the inside."

The lady looked at the glasses and she looked at him.

"Well, I guess it'll be all right," she said. "Here's your glasses."

"Thank you," he said.

It was good to know that Homeland Security could tell the difference between a real pair of Ray Ban Wayfarer sunglasses and a pair of clueless Chinese knockoffs any self-respecting sophomore at Marshall or Immaculate Heart or the Lycee International would have spotted from down the block.

***

In the morning, Harris got a cup of coffee and sat down at his computer. Typing "Starbucks career" into the Google search engine took him exactly where he wanted to go, the Starbucks Career Center.

"Would you like to work at a Starbucks?"

Fuck yeah, Harris thought. That's why I'm here.

"*Each store hires and manages its own part-time and full-time partners (employees). We're dedicated to serving ethically sourced coffee, caring for the environment and giving back to the communities where we do business.*

"*Baristas are the face of Starbucks. They create uplifting experiences for the people who visit our stores and make perfect beverages – one drink and one person at a time.*

"*Shift Supervisors are expert baristas who help direct work on the floor during shifts. They also help create great experiences for partners and customers alike.*

"*Caring for and getting to know each other, our customers and our communities is the basis of the Starbucks partner experience. There are more than 50 Partner Clubs and Networks that help our partners share interests and find work/life balance.*

"*What's it like to be a partner?*

"*Working at Starbucks is a lot like working with your friends. We understand, respect, appreciate and include different people. And we believe in keeping each other informed, so our senior leaders regularly hold Open Forum events to answer your questions.*"

It was all Harris had hoped for. And more. Friends on a journey together, giving back to the community and striking an almost Zen like balance between work and life.

He clicked the "Apply Now" icon quickly and without thinking.

***

Just in the air and already running late, Tom thought. *They'll probably hold the plane for me in Chicago, of course they will, but it will most definitely fuck things up in Los Angeles.*

What about his luggage? If you couldn't trust them to take off on time or to serve you a drink once they did take off, how the fuck could you trust them to get an unattended bag from here to there without incident? *They'll hold the plane in Chicago and my luggage may or may not be loaded into it,* he thought.

Finally, the flight attendant brought him a glass of ice and a couple flight bottles of Glenlivet and he drank and looked at his watch and outside the dark night sky didn't look any different over Ohio than it did above Illinois, Kansas or Colorado. After what seemed like forever he was back on the ground in Burbank, three thousand miles away.

"You're always fucking late," she said, grabbing the back of his head and pulling his mouth down to hers. The thrill went through him again, straight down to his crotch. He'd forgotten how tiny she was. How beautiful. He wrapped his arms around her.

"I love you," he said.

"That's your problem," she said, and she reached down and grabbed him by the balls.

CHAPTER SIX

Harris had seen green American Express cards and even gold ones, but had been unaware of the existence of the platinum cards. He looked them up as soon as he'd submitted his application.

"The American Express Platinum card is the best American Express rewards card for people with excellent credit who want a card that caters to the affluent, and for those with discerning taste," the American Express website told him.

He looked up "discerning."

"Exhibiting keen insight and good judgment; perceptive," he read. That was Angie to a T, he thought. That was her exactly.

After that first brush with her, he began hanging around the upscale but unpretentious coffee franchise, managing to be there on another occasion when she came in. Pushing his way up near to her at the cash register pretending to be looking at Starbucks gift cards, he caught her last name, Roscelli, by looking down over her shoulder when she took the card out again. He hadn't worked all those years in the retail food service business for nothing.

Having her last name allowed him to look her up on the internet, however, and what he found led him to go to Best Buy, where he bought a professional quality photographic printer so he could have pictures of her all over his apartment. He put them in frames he bought at the drugstore, simple black metal mountings meant for high school diplomas or marriage licenses, deployed now in the service of lust and lasciviousness. Pictures of Angie modeling a dress, Angie doing a scene in an old television episode opposite Jeff Daniels, Angie with her lead guitarist second husband, her aristocratic Brit third husband and all the guys before and after and in between, at nightclubs and movie openings and awards ceremonies. He knew she was somebody. And she was made for the red carpet.

There she was with Eric Burdon. Click. And David Duchovny. Click. And Dennis Wilson. Click. And Harry Dean Stanton. Click. And Todd Rundgren's ex-wife's former bass player – Click – And Dr. Jack Kervorkian.

Click.

Typing her name into Google Images in fact turned up 35,900 of them, and these were narrowed down to a few hundred on her Facebook pages. She had two of those, one for "friends" only and one for fans but there was a waiting list on the friends page because you were only allowed to have 5,000 "real" friends. He'd have to wait for someone to die to get a chance at a spot.

But Facebook was the gold mine, and now he knew which restaurants she ate at, her birthday, the sort of music she listened to, the show business celebrities she ran around with and the names of a very long list of guys who – like him – were completely devoted to her and prepared to do anything she asked of them. He knew what books she read, what movies she liked, her favorite brands of cosmetics and all about her recent vacation with her sister at San Miguel de Allende, high up in the mountains of western Mexico.

Harris spent night after night on the computer downloading images and ferreting out the various facts of her life. There was the story about her being discovered sitting on the lawn in front of Hollywood High, where she was a fifteen-year-old freshman, by the pedophile who would become her first husband. He shot himself in the head at the Chateau Marmont after a couple years, Harris read. Then there was her flight from Ireland a decade later after the gay rock star she'd married died of an overdose at his family's castle outside Ballyshannon.

There was the photo, reproduced countless times, taken at a

time when most girls her age were going out on their first date. Wearing only a dog collar, a skimpy black bra and panties, she posed on her hands and knees atop an unmade bed in what appeared to be a cheap hotel room, staring directly into the camera lens as four scruffy guys standing behind her leered wantonly. The iconic image had graced the back cover of a record album by a band that was later inducted into the Rock and Roll Hall of Fame. It drove Harris insane every time he looked at it, and he looked at it many times every day.

With all the heartache and trouble and exploitation she'd known in her life, it was no wonder that she now preferred a quiet existence, living with her little dog and walking every night to Starbucks, where she bought herself a $4.50 cup of tea before returning home and going to bed alone, he thought.

Harris also managed to find out who the older guy was, a writer named Tom Heaton, who was apparently pretty much of a drunk and a womanizer and was even still married to some woman back in New York. He'd written some books very few people had read, was in a band when he was younger and had recently been taken off a Delta Airlines flight from New York to Philadelphia after a flight attendant complained he was too drunk to fly.

Actually, there were more listings for Tom than there were for Angie, though there were far fewer pictures. The pictures showed him either as a young rocker or as a middle aged man looking just like he did when he showed up at Starbucks, dark sports coat, longish hair and sad eyes, often with a woman on his arm, a drink in his hand and always a cigarette.

What the hell did she see in him? Harris wondered. How could a writer, a dumb fuck who lived no place other than his own head, get a girl like Angie, so vital and spirited and full of life? Still, he printed out a picture of Tom – a dust jacket photo that showed him sitting at an outdoor café somewhere, looking up from a book – though Harris didn't put that one into a frame from the drugstore.

Instead he took it, along with a few sheets of biographical information he'd found on Wikipedia and Tom's publisher's website, and slid them all into a manila envelope. Know your enemy, he thought, putting the envelope into his dresser drawer.

One thing Harris never did get around to looking up was the word he'd been so enchanted with earlier, *barista*. If he had, he would have found that the noun that charmed him so had been appropriated in 1982 by a low level functionary in the public relations department at Starbucks corporate offices in Seattle.

They'd been looking for a title to bestow on their employees that would connote more prestige than "server," which is what they had been calling them previously. *Barista*, with its Old World allure and undeniable snob appeal, was simply the Italian word for "bartender."

At once it allowed customers to further rationalize their decision to pay five dollars for a cup of coffee they could have bought elsewhere for ninety-nine cents, and gave the servers themselves additional justification for having an attitude, a quality highly valued in the *faux chic* world Harris sought now to inhabit.

The mantis stalks the cricket, unaware that he is himself being stalked by the Golden Oriole.

CHAPTER SEVEN

"What are you doing?" she asked. Sometimes the simple question bears fruit that a more intense examination cannot reveal, Tom thought.

She didn't really care what he was doing, the question was put for no reason other than to illustrate that whatever he was doing at that particular moment wasn't as important as what she wanted him to do.

What he had been doing was staring at a largely blank white computer screen, sullied only by two paragraphs of roughly fifty words apiece that represented for him that morning's entire literary output. He'd started on a novel about Hollywood and the commodification of fame; a smutty book, noirish, ironic and cynical in outlook yet appallingly commercial in intent.

His mind had been groping helplessly for the sentence, the word, that would begin the next paragraph in some sort of reasonable fashion, in a style that successfully disguised calculation and complexity as innocence and sincerity while at the same time conveying a profound understanding of the human condition, when some potatoes in the kitchen sink needed peeling and she asked what he was doing and suddenly he wasn't doing anything at all. They argued and he went into the bedroom and fell fast asleep. When he woke up, a couple hours before dawn, she was gone.

He'd taken an apartment in the hills overlooking the intersection of Hollywood and Sunset, on Talmadge Avenue in a house that dated back to a time when one could reasonably name a building the "Gardens of Allah" without having to worry about possible terrorists reprisals. There was a courtyard in front with boulders and bamboo trees and an artfully gnarled white alder, and the street itself was named after Norma Talmadge, the biggest star Vitagraph Studios had during the silent era. The old studio, now given over to daytime soap opera production and run by Disney, stretched for a city block below the terrace out back.

A billboard visible on the far side of the studio advertised a hotel on Sunset Boulevard. "We're so Hollywood, our pool should be shallow at both ends," it said.

Beyond that rose the low green hills, dotted with millionaires' mansions facing the sunset west. The way the slope rose slowly and the thick palm trees and the constant drone of police and television station helicopters coming in low over the crest reminded him of Vietnam the way it was portrayed in the film *Apocalypse Now*. In his mind, Tom mounted various military campaigns aimed at capturing the summit.

All in all it was a satisfactory place to live in Los Angeles, upscale without being ostentatious, and he lived there with the old black Chihuahua Rowena, and was comfortable. She'd given him the dog so he wouldn't be lonely when she wasn't there, she said, but in reality it was Rowena who made the decision. After staying at Tom's place for a couple of nights, the dog showed a marked preference for the steaks Tom cooked for her than to the vegan fare Angie served at her former residence.

On the roof of one of the soundstages that made up the old Vitagraph Studios, a pair of ravens had made their nest and Tom watched them every day as the father guarded the chicks while the mother went out and brought back food. The nest was partially obscured by the deep gutter it was built in, but appeared to be about five feet long. The big black birds swaggered around it on foot or rolled and somersaulted in the sky above.

Out back that night, in the overgrown dry wash that ran down the hill and separated the lot of his building from that of the studio, a coyote yipped and howled in the darkness and the dog shot up in her bed, ears pointed and craning her neck to see out the window. Rowena looked over at him, sitting at his desk reading, and ran across the room and jumped up into his lap.

"It's all right, girl," he said, petting her. "He's out there and we're in here."

For the time being, he thought to himself.

***

On Christmas Day Tom sat poolside on a plush chaise lounge in the backyard of a big house belonging to one of Angie's girlfriends, Gretchen Bonaduce, a reality television star whose show had recently been cancelled. It was hot in the sun and he'd taken off the black silk sport coat he'd worn, and he sipped on a glass of bubbling Veuve Clicquot.

There were young girls parading around in string bikinis and heavyset older women who had the power to make or break an up and comer and the ex-wives of famous or formerly famous rock stars, along with a goodly number of unattached and casually dressed men of various ages and bank balances.

Angie told him their hostess, Gretchen, got the place as part of the divorce settlement she'd received from her ex-husband, Danny Bonaduce, who – as a child – had starred in a long running television series called "The Partridge Family," and who until recently had been her costar on the cancelled reality show.

The reality show centered on Danny's sometimes happy and sometimes sad but always poignant attempts to quit drinking and doing drugs and Gretchen's busy life raising two kids, shopping on Rodeo Drive and undergoing a series of plastic surgeries that left her with the face and body of a woman who would never be mistaken for a truck stop waitress from Indiana, which is what Angie said she had been before she met

37

Danny, who did not attend the party himself.

He had, in fact, taken a job around Thanksgiving as the morning man on Seattle radio station KZOK, where listeners were treated to rants about how his ex-wife and her musician boyfriend Kevin were living off Gretchen's alimony and child support payments in Danny's old manse, and how he'd paid for her boobs and lips and eyes and other cosmetic surgeries.

Now Gretchen said she had to put the place on the market because she couldn't afford to pay the taxes on it since the show had been cancelled, which was kind of ironic. They probably should have made a show about that.

But Tom wasn't thinking about Gretchen and her cancelled reality show. From behind the dark sunglasses he wore he watched as a shifty dago named Joel chatted Angie up over by the diving board.

The guy was one of six session drummers who played on Debbie Gibson's 1987 "Out of the Blue" album and then spent the next twenty-five years telling people he was a musician. More recently, he told people he was an actor too, having appeared in a video short shot by a friend of his up in Griffith Park.

In reality, he was a two-bit hustler who sold cheap camera junk imported from the former Soviet block to flyover state film students on eBay. Tom knew what he was and didn't like him.

"You never call anymore," Joel said to Angie. "I get the feeling you don't like me."

She was the sexiest woman he'd ever known. Sex oozed from her pores and her dreamy green eyes put him into a hypnotic trance.

"I told you I'm seeing somebody," she said sweetly, shooting a nervous look over at Tom, who was lighting a cigarette. Joel leaned in, putting one hand past her shoulder and onto the base of the diving board.

"So what's that? That means you forget about all your old

friends? We used to have a lot of fun."

He kissed her on the cheek as she turned her head.

"Everybody always said we looked so good together Angie," he said.

She looked over again towards Tom but he was gone. Then she looked back at Joel and was horrified to see Tom standing right behind him.

"No…" she started, but it was too late.

"Hey, Giuseppe," Tom said in a loud voice, and as Joel turned Tom caught him in the temple with his fist, which was clenched around the heavy switchblade knife he brought with him from New York. As quick as he could, Tom struck his man another blow in the same spot, and Joel crumpled to the porphyry paving stones that lined the area around the pool. Like Joel's own grandfather, the stones had been imported from Italy and he fell on them and bled on them just as he would have if they were all back home.

"What are you doing?" Angie screamed, but Tom heard her only tangentially as he took a step back and delivered a vicious kick to Joel's midsection.

Joel let out a sick, choked scream as the hornback head cut alligator toe of Tom's boot dug home and cracked a rib.

All around the pool people stopped talking and the only sounds you could hear were the breeze blowing through the trees and Joel's pathetic moaning. Angie sat on her haunches next to him and looked pleadingly up at Tom, who thought of how much it looked like that picture they show of the kid shot dead at Kent State all those years ago and the chick squatting down next to him crying.

Tom wasn't a tough guy, not in the sense of the tough guys he'd known in Detroit or Brooklyn or Mexico City. But the day he'd take shit from a musician or a fucking actor hadn't yet arrived.

In any event, he decided against breaking Joel's nose with

his heel, didn't want her to see that so close up and didn't want Joel to enrich the fucking plastic surgeons over on Wilshire any more than he already had.

He turned and walked away from the pool and down the long driveway that led to the street. When he got there he put his knife away and lit a cigarette and headed over to Sunset, where he could find a bar to disappear into and call a cab.

He was almost to the corner when Angie pulled up next to him in her big silver Escalade. He kept walking and she touched the button for the window as she rolled alongside him.

"What are you, a sick fucking animal?" she yelled at him. "He didn't even do anything."

Tom kept walking.

"The police are coming," she said. "Get in the car."

"You let that fucking guy kiss you? Right in front of me?"

"Get in the car."

She stopped and he got in and at the intersection an ambulance sped through past them and towards the scene of the crime.

Angie threw the car into park and before he knew what was happening she was straddling him with her legs, locking her arms around the back of his neck, pressing her open lips against his and shoving her tongue into his mouth.

"God I love you so much," she said.

"I love you too baby," he said, squeezing a perfect firm breast with his hand and kissing her back.

The light changed twice and even through her tights and his jeans he felt her pussy, hot and wet, rubbing up and down against his hard cock.

"I think we're holding up traffic," he said, and she bit him savagely on the lower lip and he tasted the blood.

A couple cars rolled past them and the drivers yelled things they couldn't hear and Angie dismounted him the way you would a horse swinging back into the driver's seat.

"We're going to Malibu," she said, putting the car in gear and making a sharp right. "I know a place."

They drove west all the way through the city on Sunset. Angie wouldn't drive the freeways.

It was dark and cool when they checked into their bungalow and he could hear the surf and the waning moon lit the whole thing up in a creepy white light. It was a crescent moon, falling away from the evening star of Venus.

***

Sometimes it seemed like a big wind had come through, blowing all the impurities out of the air for him and leaving just a crystalline view of what was waiting in the distance, what could be his for the taking.

The morning sun was bright and the air was warm and the thought of Gretchen's party and what happened there seemed unreal to him. He drank his coffee and smoked and for a moment he felt alone in what seemed to be a beautiful universe created for no reason other than his own edification.

Down below, the waves were breaking on Zuma Beach and the palm trees swayed in the breeze. Out back, the mountain rose green, willow and poplar and tall grasses of every description decorated with wildflowers, violet or white, yellow and red. In the blue sky above, an enormous hawk moved in the wind, motionless but for its currents, up or down, forward and back.

Tom had stayed in better hotels, but never one built into the side of a mountain overlooking the Pacific Ocean and a beach Neil Young named an album after. There was a graceful severity about the place he found comforting. The sound of a barking dog blew in on the warm ocean breeze.

She walked out onto the deck and into the sun wearing her sunglasses and an old black silk robe a different girl had given him a decade before. When he looked up, she let the robe drop to the floor and her white skin, beautiful but lurid, glowed ethereal, reflecting in the light. He tossed the cigarette he'd been smoking into the little stream that ran down alongside.

"You're killing me," he said.

"You're gonna die anyway," she replied, walking toward him slow so he could take it all in. They kissed deeply and he put his arms around her, holding her so tight he was afraid for a moment she might break.

"You wanna fuck me baby?" she said rubbing his cock, and he picked her up in both arms and carried her back into the darkened room.

Inside she felt like cashmere, hot wet cashmere wrapping him up and driving any thought of this fucked up world from his mind forever. He was consumed by her, lost in her, oblivious to the passing of time or even his own identity, crazy, tumbling, psychotic and tender. She squirmed beneath him.

Afterwards, they sat out on the deck in the Jacuzzi, the water almost scalding, her lying back in his arms, him smoking a Lucky Strike and drinking from a cold bottle of Pacifico, quiet and aloof.

If happiness is pleasure he was happy then.

In the coral sky to the west, out over the vast ocean itself, a shooting star burned up in the atmosphere.

"I love you," he said at last.

"Don't say that," she said, staring at the redwood fence in front of them. "Don't say that to me anymore."

So he shut up, and they sat like that until it got dark, and they both started to fall asleep.

***

Her life was a teenage fantasy. Nobody else was like her, no one felt things as deeply as she did and nobody wanted or

42

dreamed or struggled as she had. Other people got a mosquito bite but Angie got West Nile Virus. She was the central figure in a high drama of her own creation. The star of the show.

He was much the same, delusional about his own ambition and destiny to the point that he had, to a large degree, managed to create a tiny universe in which he actually could be who he imagined himself to be.

In his mind, he was playing for the highest stakes imaginable – Immortality. He saw himself sitting at the table with Stephen Crane and Jane Bowles, Delmore Schwartz, Flannery O'Connor, Jack London and Jim Thompson, with all of them from all of history who thought that maybe they could do one good thing, one thing better than themselves. That they could do one thing nobody else could since nobody else had seen and heard and done the things they had, hadn't experienced life in the same way, and who somehow managed to set a tiny sliver of it down on paper so exactly and so perfectly as to illuminate some immaculate truth, a truth so timeless and universal it would live forever and – by extension – carry its discoverer's name on with it.

For Tom and Angie, these fantasies and delusions were nothing more or less than survival strategies, and they lived in a world where things and people and ideas existed only in relation to what they thought about them.

The books he'd written, the handful of films she made and the hundreds of cheesecake photos that littered her Google Image Search were what separated them from the mass of people, the ones who only dreamed about doing things, talked about them without acting, afraid of their own shadows, waiting around for somebody to tell them what to do. The nothing people who lived vicariously through *Dancing with the Stars* or *America's Got Talent* and struggled to make ends meet. The ones who never went anywhere or knew anyone or did anything remarkable and thought that who they voted for

43

President actually mattered.

"I love it when you talk to me… about me," she said, lying beside him in bed the next morning.

Later that afternoon she called Gretchen, who said she should have known better than to invite Joel when she knew Angie was bringing Tom.

"I don't know what I was thinking," she said.

The cops had been there and Joel was taken away in an ambulance. Nobody said anything. It must have been some party crasher or something was the story everybody told. Joel would be OK. They hadn't even kept him all night.

Tom was disappointed. He was hoping he'd given the little prick a concussion, at least.

They went down for a light lunch on the patio looking out toward Catalina and afterward took a long walk on the beach toward Point Dume.

"That's where they shot the end of 'Planet of the Apes,'" she said, pointing to the cliff.

Tom dropped down to his knees.

"YOU MANIACS!!!!" he shouted, pounding his fist in the sand. 'YOU BLEW IT UP!!!! GOD DAMN YOU!!!! GOD DAMN YOU ALL TO HELL…."

CHAPTER EIGHT

Tony was always talking shit. He'd go on and on about how Jimmy Carter hadn't invented the word "malaise" but after the media started calling a nationally televised address he gave in 1979 the "Malaise Speech," people at least became aware of the word, what it meant and how to pronounce it and – even today, all these years later – you still heard it used from time to time on *MSNBC* or saw it in the paper once in awhile if you read the paper.

But that afternoon, his focus was on philosophy rather than etymology or political science.

"The world makes liars of us all," he said, and Harris looked at him annoyed. They sat at the dark bar of the Drawing Room on Hillhurst in Los Feliz, light streaming in from the open door.

Tony never took his eyes off his own reflection in the mirror behind the bar. He was fifty-two years old and played bass in a band that had a regular Saturday night gig at the Silver Lake Farmer's Market on Sunset. Their guitar player's brother served on the Silver Lake Community Advisory Board so they got to play every Saturday night and each guy brought home two hundred fifty dollars. It was better than nothing.

Back in the 70s, he'd recorded and toured with the Starland Vocal Band, a group well known for an utter inability to play their own instruments. He'd been in the right place at the right time and the money had been so good he was able to buy the house in Beachwood Canyon that he still lived in.

He sipped his stale Brotherhood Ale, the artisanal beer they made over in Atwater Village with water from the Los Angeles River. Ratwater, Harris called it, but Tony didn't care. Bread, beer, whatever; it didn't matter to him. Tony was all about artisanal. He even did his shopping at Whole Foods. The chicks loved it.

"What's wrong with you?" Harris said. "What the hell are you even talking about?"

Tony had lately noticed a certain edginess coming over his friend, an edginess Harris wasn't quite able to pull off. He'd taken to wearing sunglasses indoors, even in dimly lit dives like the Drawing Room.

"I realize you bring a lifetime of learning to bear on the subject, and I have only my ignorance and a certain simple objectivity," Tony said. "But I gotta think that, no matter what a person's intentions are, the world has a way of turning it around and showing you that all your promises and good intentions don't mean shit."

Harris downed the last of his Black Velvet and motioned for the barmaid to bring him another. She was short and blonde and chunky and she dressed like a prostitute. Her nose had been broken at some time in the past and hadn't healed quite right. She was the kind of girl Harris might have gone out with a couple of months earlier and Tony was still trying to nail.

"The world doesn't do anything," Harris said wearily. "It's people. Either they make things happen or they let things happen to them. Most people are professional victims."

"But not you, huh?"

"You're goddamn right not me."

"So what makes you so different?" Tony asked.

"I got plans, my man. I got plans."

Harris thought of Starbucks.

And he thought of Angie.

***

The freaks come out at night, and in Tom's neighborhood they came out where Vermont and Hollywood and Sunset all intersected, that ghetto fabulous triple corner on the edge of nowhere with the cab stands and the *taqueria* and the Rite Aid and the Bank of America and Starbucks. She wanted to go for her latte and he didn't feel like it. His knee was bothering him. He'd busted it up many years ago in a car crash then re-injured it many times over the years and now it had gotten to where a snap of cold weather or rain could all but cripple him and walking too much on any given day might spell disaster whether it was cold and rainy or not.

His bad knee annoyed her and was on her list as one of the many things she put up with because she loved him so much. But he'd get in a foul mood when it acted up and, a couple weeks earlier in San Francisco, where they'd gone for a reading and book signing event, he became upset when she actually had a wheelchair waiting for him at the airport.

He didn't like her going down there alone at night like that, he worried about her, but it was four miles round trip and when he did go the knee was often swollen and bad the next day. He said he'd drive her and she said no, she'd walk with Rowena and he was too tired to argue with her. He was starting to feel old.

He hated that thirty years of hard living was finally beginning to catch up with him – the smoking and the drinking, the broken bones and knocked out teeth, the guilt and the frustration and the rage. The rage that never went away no matter how much money he made or how many women he took to bed. Always simmering, just beneath the surface.

***

She went there the same time every night, usually around nine o'clock, sometimes alone and sometimes with that asshole writer Heaton and the little black dog. Harris would wait until he saw her alone and then take a table near hers on the patio outside. She'd sip her Chai latte and talk on the iPhone she always carried. It rang constantly, playing an old rock song he didn't know.

Tonight, she and the dog arrived without Heaton, and Harris wondered about that, hoping against hope that he would never again see the asshole, who so obviously didn't deserve her.

"*I remember when she got her facelift...*" Angie told whomever she was talking to on the phone.

"*But that's different. It's not like you're going in there every six weeks...*"

"*So maybe it's eight weeks. I don't know, but I'm not going to have them put botulism in me...*" she said.

Harris leaned in sideways to eavesdrop, his eyes looking straight ahead. He was wearing a pair of Levis and a black shirt.

He'd made a mental note to himself to buy more black shirts but hadn't gotten around to it yet and now just had the one. The baristas at Starbucks had black shirts issued to them, he thought, and he wondered sometimes how he could have lived so long and not realized that black was the best color there was for clothes.

She wore black, of course. A short, flouncy pleated skirt and opaque black stockings, knee high suede boots with spiked heels and a kind of tight lacy top that pushed her small firm breasts up almost even with her shoulders. Over that she wore a black school blazer with brass buttons. Her long black hair looked as if she'd just gotten out of bed, out of a bed where she hadn't been sleeping, and the white skin of her face, almost translucent, augmented with just a touch of dark lipstick and maybe a little something around the eyes. It was hard to tell.

"*I mean, there's so many products on the market...*" she said. "*I understand if you're one of those girls, actresses, who make their money on being beautiful...*"

"... *But Bette Davis was a huge film star! She was a real actress!*"

He hung on her every word. He didn't know who she was talking to or what they were talking about but, to him, whatever it was, it was the most fascinating thing in the world. He wanted to know everything about her, what made her tick, how she came to be, her essence and the color of her soul.

"*Everybody wants to look like Angelina Jolie but unless you look like Angelina Jolie -- like six feet tall, a hundred pounds – I'm sorry, but those big lips just look bad...*"

"*I'm telling you right now I'd look stupid if my lips were any bigger. They wouldn't fit my face...*"

With her delicate hands, she was breaking the blueberry scone he'd watched her buy into small pieces and feeding them to the little dog who stood on the ground at her feet, putting the smallest pieces into her own mouth.

"*Mmm-mmm...Mmm-mmm...*"

"*...You're letting your hair grow out now? Yeah, I know, me too... I hate it...*

"*Right... She told me she could make my body look like sixteen again... I said could I just lay there while you do it? She said no, you've got to do the work... I said fuck that shit.*"

Harris was happy Angie's telephone friend wasn't sitting at the table with her. He didn't care what she had to say but, more than that, someone else sitting there would certainly have noticed his efforts to eavesdrop.

All that mattered was that he was ten feet away from the most beautiful woman in Hollywood, whose scent was that of the deepest sexual desire and whose emerald green eyes promised a knowing carnality far beyond any simple sensuality he had ever experienced.

"*Does Daryl Hannah even work anymore...?*"

"*Yeah, you saw her after Pearl Jam... Remember, she was at Harvey's thing at the Whiskey?*

"Is it her line of makeup...?

"Yeah, yeah. Yeah, too bad...

"I love her hair...

"She's always been a really sweet kid, independent, that's what I love about her... Yeah...

"Who was that French director, what was his name? I've forgotten his name...

"Yeah... Now he wants to control her life, put her on a pedestal..."

She got up from the table and bent over to untangle Rowena's pink leash from the wrought iron leg of one of the chairs. A flash of gartered white thigh and Harris thought he would explode in his pants.

"But she fell in love with him, what are you going to do? I don't know... it depends on the guy. How do you answer that?

"You've got to be open to the possibility..."

She dropped her cup into the receptacle and walked away up Prospect, out of earshot and back toward the hills. He thought of following her but didn't. One night he would, he promised himself, but tonight wasn't the night.

Instead he walked over to where she'd been sitting and, spying a piece of blueberry scone the dog had somehow missed lying on the ground, picked it up and put it to his nose. Eyes closed, he smelled the sweet blueberries and pictured her in his mind.

"Of course she's emotional, her mom's dead..." he heard her say from down the street, her voice fading.

Harris dared to dream. In his reverie, he imagined Angie at his place, sitting on the couch and watching her shows on TV, or in the morning at the kitchen counter, fixing herself something for breakfast. Then he saw her in his bedroom, on his bed, her legs slightly spread...

He opened his eyes and ate the piece of blueberry scone, the piece she'd broken off with her own delicate fingers, the piece she'd meant for her dog, and tasted the juicy sweetness for himself.

In the dark sky above, Orion the Hunter looked down on a world full of pain. But Harris felt none of it and he went home savoring the taste of the blueberries and remembering the flash of Angie's creamy thigh.

When he got back to his apartment in Glendale, he lie down on his bed and jacked off just thinking about it.

CHAPTER NINE

There was more to it than that, of course.

In the oddly blended mixture of Buddhism and Shintoism that constitutes organized religion throughout much of Japan, there is a belief that old and thrown away objects, after a certain period of time, became possessed by demons angered by their casual abandonment. These were the unspeakable *tsukumogami*.

"Unlike the mortals who had discarded them, the vengeful specters were having a great time celebrating and feasting – building a castle out of flesh and creating a blood fountain. They danced and drank, boasting that even celestial pleasures could not surpass their own," Tom read, and he thought of Rachel, alone and far away in New York.

"'We have faithfully served the houses as furniture and utensils for a long time. But instead of getting the reward that is our due, we are abandoned in the alleys to be kicked by oxen and horses. Insult has been added to injury, and this is the greatest insult of all! Whatever it takes, we should become specters and exact vengeance.'"

Tom's studies into the esoteric Shingon Buddhism had taken a sudden and somewhat disturbing turn. The *tsukumogami* and their damnable shrine in the recesses of Mount Funaoka, that dark temple to the Great Shape-Shifting God called Henge Daimyojin by the old Shinto priests.

He remembered the ancient city of Kyoto, in the shadow of that haunted mountain, and his own failings and the many things over which he had no control. It had been his first and only trip to Japan.

Alive and self aware, the *tsukumogami* could take the form of men or women, young or old, of the inanimate objects they once were or of beasts such as ravens and coyotes.

There had once been an occasion, you know, a hundred

years ago it seemed to Tom now, when driving that white Camaro – car weighed but eighteen hundred pounds and had a three-fifty four barrel under the hood – at a high rate of speed along an ice-covered country road very late one snowy night, drunker than hell and heading home from the small town in Pennsylvania where he served as chief editor of the little daily newspaper they had there, when he hit a particularly slippery patch of black ice and the car spun out, winding up in a ravine some twenty feet beneath the roadway, near a small stream they called Hare Creek.

He hadn't been injured and he climbed up out of the ravine back to the roadway and, just then, a drinking buddy happened to be driving by in an old green Ford F-150 pickup truck and stopped. Tom got in and they went back into town and had a few more drinks before someone else gave him a ride back to his house in the country.

The next day he learned that he had been charged by the town police – who had discovered his car – with numerous violations, including driving too fast for conditions and leaving the scene of an accident.

When he went in to see the chief of police the following Monday, a part of his normal duties as chief editor of the local newspaper, the chief got up from behind his desk and closed the door.

"Now this is strictly off the record, Tom," he said, sitting back down. "But my man told me he drove down that road, got to the intersection outside of town, turned around and drove back. Between that time, which he said couldn't have been more than a minute or two, your car was not there and then it was there but you were not. He doesn't like you, Tom, and he looked for you for the rest of his shift, in the cruiser and on foot, but he still couldn't find you.

"Now, what I want to know is… How in the hell did you do that?"

Tom took a sip of the bitter black coffee from the Styrofoam cup.

"Well Dana…" The police chief's name was Dana Scouten and the two were on a first name basis. "What happened was this: I knew your man was on the lookout for me, so when I slid off the roadway like that I just turned myself into a coyote and skinned up along the creek bed toward home. I knew he'd be looking for a man and not a dog."

For a minute the police chief stared blankly, but then he began to laugh. He laughed uproariously.

"I'm gonna miss you when you go, Tom," he said, wiping his eye and sighing.

It had all happened so long ago, and Tom had bent his mind in so many different ways during the intervening years, that now the story of a drinking buddy just happening along some lonely country road at two o'clock in the morning that night seemed every bit as unlikely as the one about him turning himself into a coyote.

"*Like a string of rosary beads, my mind cannot be severed from angry thoughts,*" he read.

He poured a belt of Glenlivet into the highball glass on the nightstand and drank. The book, Elizabeth Lillehoj's *Transfiguration: Man-made Objects as Demons in Japanese Scrolls*, a book he had sitting on his shelves for years but was somehow just now getting around to reading, fell down on his covered belly.

He remembered Kyoto and looked over at the fourteenth century mounted katana, his souvenir from that trip, and he thought of the shape shifters and that time back in Pennsylvania.

Like the great thief, Dao Zhi, who followed the five cardinal Confucian virtues, the evil and violent specters believed that piety would outweigh their malevolent transgressions. And so did Tom, sometimes.

The dog Rowena slept on the thick red comforter beside him, breathing in and out, dreaming the dreams of an old soul. With his fingertips he stroked the top of her skull, where the dark hairs were turning silver much like his own.

Outside in the night, beneath what they were calling the "Super Moon of 2012" because of its close proximity to earth, it began to rain, and then the rain turned into a torrential downpour.

The mated ravens, who had built their shambling five-foot nest into a gutter between the roofs of two of the soundstages at the old Vitagraph Studios right behind his house watched helplessly as the runoff carried their nest and their young flightless chicks off and into a sewer that ran into the open cistern they called the Los Angeles River.

Everything for nothing.

Yin and yang. Life and death, the same. He scratched Rowena's head and closed his eyes. He wondered about Angie, who was on the other side of the river, exhausted and sleeping.

The overhead light was on, and he was too tired to get up and turn it off. He made a mental note to get himself a lamp for the nightstand, maybe something vintage, with a shade made from panes of colored glass.

He hated sleeping alone and was glad for the dog. He thought of the ravens crying their raven cries over the deaths of their babies.

***

It was Angie's massage therapist, Renata, who first began planting the seeds of doubt.

"I told you, falling for a married drunk who lived three thousand miles away was just crazy," Renata said. "But you wouldn't listen. You never listen."

"Oh shut up Renata."

55

"You remember what happened at Gretchen's party? Well, that's gonna come your way someday."

"Shut up, Renata. Really. Shut up."

"Once a cheater, always a cheater," Renata said. "I learned that the hard way, believe me. If he left one wife for you, you can expect that he will do the same to you someday."

"Renata..."

"I know. Shut up. Fine. Don't listen to me then. You'll find out for yourself. You wait and see."

They'd had a fight, Tom snapped and swore at her when she said something about his drinking after San Francisco, and the next morning he put the dog into the old Cadillac and just started driving. When she called that night, Tom told her he was about one hundred miles east of Reno, barreling down Route 80 on his way to Battle Mountain, where he was hoping to photograph the wild horse herd and clear his head.

Now Angie was miserable and despondent and, eight hundred miles away in the high desert of northern Nevada, so was Tom. He was having car trouble as well.

"so alone....really broken now. will spend night fixing flat tire in freezing rain. i love you so much...no idea how i could exist without you, or even if that is possible....no. clearly that is not possible," he wrote.

She replied almost instantly. Like she'd been waiting.

"your words mean nothing to me anymore.....your actions say everything.......if you want to make changes to better your life then do it.....otherwise your life is lived through the eyes of an alcoholic and a liar....neither one interest me.....if you want to kill yourself, i won't stand by and watch.....prove it to me before it's too late......this is your last chance......your next drink just might be your last."

The car limped into Battle Mountain sometime after four in the morning and Tom knew it was going to need some major work in order to get it back on the road. He took a room at the

Lucky Nugget Casino and drank until they wouldn't serve him anymore.

The rain had stopped. Walking back to his room, he paused to watch a passenger train in the distance, all silver cars and lighted windows, snaking its way from west to east across the Great Basin and heading toward Salt Lake City along the old Central Pacific line. He wished he was on that train.

All his life he'd been a highly functioning alcoholic who had never had much trouble finding men to pay him money for his work and women to sleep with him for free. Still, all of the jobs ended up with him getting fired over the drinking, and all the relationships ended in bitter recrimination.

The cirrhosis diagnosis six years ago came as no surprise to him or anyone else. Incurable and always fatal, the disease had lived inside him for so long now he had come to regard it as a distant though ultimately reliable friend. Tom knew their day of reckoning would come but – before Angie – he hadn't cared much about it one way or the other.

Another sick thing he had inside him was the rage, a savage anger that had been there ever since he was a kid. He didn't know where it came from or what to do about it. It only came out now when he was drinking, but since he was pretty much drinking all the time it was never far below the surface. Now Angie had seen it and it scared her to death.

He thought about these things, these mysteries, lying on the bed in his hotel room, the television on but muted and Rowena sleeping beside him, pushing up as close as she could for warmth. He scratched her tired head and told her she was the best dog in the world and was happy Angie had been thoughtful enough to hang a medallion engraved with her home address and telephone number on it from the dog's collar.

Just in case.

"as usual it's all about you and the drama you create," she wrote. *"if you want a better life and better relationships.......then do the changes it requires.....stop hiding behind your past and making excuses for everything you don't like about your life.....how about being present for the life you say u love more than god....step up and take responsibility for the shit you've created and make the changes needed to have a better life and become a better man....or just keep hiding behind the bottle,"* she wrote.

The next day he woke feeling like death itself. He opened the hotel room door and squinted in the bright high desert sunlight. He had a headache from the booze and he had a headache from the mile-high altitude on top of that. Down in the parking lot below, the Cadillac – in need of two tires, a ball joint and perhaps as many as four shock absorbers, sat bleaching.

Black-billed magpies cavorted among the pines over by the swimming pool and mocked him. They were big birds, eighteen inches long at least, and their black and white plumage stood out against the dull landscape and even from the lush green of the pines that required constant watering and attention in that harsh climate.

The magpies seemed comfortable in the thin air and, like Tom himself, were opportunistic omnivores who would even eat garbage and flesh despite their intelligence and striking good looks. They made him think of the ravens back in Los Angeles and even of that big hawk, drifting and dropping in the breeze above Malibu.

He couldn't get her out of his head. She was Lilith and Salome, Delilah, Cleopatra and Helen of Troy, Morgan le Fay, de Sade's Juliette, Emma Bovary and Mata Hari all rolled into one. She consumed his imagination.

Angelique. No matter where he ran he couldn't get away from her. Angie. She lived inside him now and would forever. Was it a curse or a blessing? He couldn't say.

He went back in and made some coffee. He couldn't eat, but he ordered up a New York strip for Rowena. Medium well, no vegetables, no potato. The toothless old woman who brought it up, Colleen, her name was, played with Rowena on the floor of the room and looked like some long lost impoverished relative of his so Tom tipped her three times as much as was necessary. He called the automobile club and had the car towed to the town's lone Cadillac dealership. They told him it would take two and a half days to get the parts in, and that FedEx and UPS didn't deliver there on the weekends.

Battle Mountain was a pretty spot – all juniper and pinyon trees, cheap bars, legal whorehouses and a few small casinos set at the confluence of the Humboldt and Reese rivers – and if he hadn't been madlessly in love with his Hollywood glamour girl girlfriend it would have been as good a place as any to drink himself to death, which is what the plan might have been in the first place.

He couldn't remember, really.

To the south, a range of low brown hills, not unlike those back in Hollywood, rose to their heights and beyond that, the rugged snow capped peaks of the Ruby Mountains, rocky and grey, challenged the countryside. Between the two ranges were the wild horse herds, which could be detected at a distance by the cloud of dust they kicked up every time they moved. In the noonday sun, the temperature approached ninety degrees. But in the night, the mercury fell below forty and he put on a sweatshirt.

"the best part of you was me....and everything i tried was to help you be the man you wanted....but at the end of the day you are who you are."

No matter where he was, she had to get the last word in.

***

59

When Angie and her sister Chloe and their mother went shopping and to lunch at the Americana at Brand in Glendale, she didn't say a word about the problems she and Tom were having. Instead she bought some cosmetics she wouldn't use and had a grilled chicken salad with avocado and sipped a big glass of cranberry with lime at the Granville Café. They all seemed bright and happy.

***

Tom didn't drink that third day, and he didn't drink the next day either. Instead he sweated it out and laid in bed watching his hands shake, getting up only occasionally to vomit. He'd order up steak or hamburger for Rowena and bottle after bottle of Pellegrino for himself.

"talked to the car dealership, they said the parts will be here tomorrow," he wrote…*"i will drive for fourteen hours and be home as fast as i can….when i get there, I'll go to rehab, join aa, see a shrink, whatever you want….i'm not drinking today, if you want to talk… please don't leave me angelique….love forever, t."*

He slept restlessly for a few hours then woke. She'd written back.

"this is not over….it will never be over….until one of us dies and probably not even then….our love will haunt us forever….pick our love and a new chapter in life….i gave you the best book you ever wrote….because of who i am and what we r together…..your journey here has been amazing and hard….but you have had an experience like no other….felt things you never felt….learned things about yourself you didn't know…..all because you decided you wanted something more something better….you did it….don't let it slip away….you're stronger than that….you tom fucking heaton…. i need you to be strong for me and for us…..i love you."

She called him late that night and they talked until dawn. He loved her and she loved him. There was nothing either of

60

them could do about it. She was right, he told her. It wouldn't be over when one of them died, it wouldn't even be over when both of them died. Because then they'd just pick up where they left off somewhere else.

"Tell me how much you love me, Tom," she said.

"I love you more than life itself, Angie," he told her. "I love you more than God."

And it was true.

CHAPTER TEN

No one knows the day or hour. And uneasy lays the head that wears the crown. Or some shit like that. Right?

Harris had a little zip in his step as he got ready to go into work that morning. Just yesterday afternoon he'd gotten the call from Starbucks, a month after handing in his application.

It was a beautiful sunny morning as he drove down Colorado toward his Jack in the Box, and on the way he stopped off to have his car washed and detailed.

The team leaders and assistant managers and team members marveled at his mood. They'd never seen him like this before. He smiled and called them by name, and he pitched in when they got a little shorthanded at the drive-through window during the noontime rush.

"What a beautiful day," he said, time after time, looking out at the brown hills beneath the baby blue Southern California sky. One of the team leaders, Joachim, joked that Harris's doctors must have finally found the right combination of meds.

He was even pleasant to the customers.

"Bacon milkshake? Mmmm…" he said. "I think I'll have one of those myself when my shift's over."

He'd scheduled a personal day for the interview, and gone out a day earlier to buy some new clothes at the J.C. Penny store in the Americana. Like it was a sign from God, he saw Angie, with two other women he barely noticed.

They were walking towards him and when he tried to make eye contact and smile, it actually worked! Angie returned his gaze and smiled back. She wondered if she knew him from some place. She knew a lot of people, of course, and even people she didn't know thought they knew her, so she always tried to be gracious.

Harris tripped on the toe of his shoe, stumbled and recovered, then wondered if she'd seen. She had. Actually, she'd seen it hundreds of times. She had made men nervous her whole life. Men without poise or courage, money or fame, the vast majority of men for whom a woman like her was an untouchable fantasy.

Recovering, he looked back to catch a glimpse of her ass before remembering the purpose of his mission. Clothes make the man, and he'd learned the importance of designer labels. When he saw the black Christian Audigier woven shirt on the sales rack for just fourteen dollars, he knew he had to have it. He'd never heard of Audigier – nobody had, actually – but he didn't really know much about fashion designers and figured one French sounding name was just as good as another.

For pants he picked a pair of black Dockers signature slim-fit, even though with his thirty-four-inch waist they seemed like they might be a little too slim fitting, and they pushed up on his crotch. The pants set him back thirty-seven dollars, but you've got to spend money to make money, he thought.

The boots and sport coat he bought – which raised his total to a whopping three hundred, sixty-one dollars after tax – were witless copies of the ones he'd seen Tom Heaton wear on his nighttime Starbucks excursions with Angie. He went home and pressed the pants and the shirt, carefully cutting off the tags and hanging the new clothes up in the hall closet so they wouldn't be contaminated by the Jack in the Box wear that filled his bedroom closet.

Then he sat down on the couch and poured himself a glass of Black Velvet and settled in to watch "Keeping Up with the Kardashians," a show about the rich and famous that never did seem to explain why they were famous or how they managed to become rich.

Tonight was the sixteenth birthday of Kendall or Kylie, he couldn't really keep those two straight, but he expected everything would go wrong, which was usually what happened on "Keeping Up with the Kardashians." The sisters were all pretty hot and he liked watching them strutting around in their different outfits.

To Harris, there was absolutely no qualitative difference between Kim Kardashian and Meryl Streep. They were both on television. In fact, when he watched Meryl accepting her umpteenth Academy Award a few weeks earlier, he thought she looked kind of old and clunky.

Kim, on the other hand, looked kind of like a bigger version of Angie, dark and sexy, her fashion sense never off kilter. A bit younger, of course.

"Celebrity Rehab" was another show that pleased him because it demonstrated that having once been on a television show or in a band was no ticket to real happiness. Most of those people were miserable, he thought. But he was waiting for this week's episode because it was part two of a special two-parter he'd started watching last week.

"In part two of this special two-part edition of Celebrity Rehab Revisited, Dr. Drew and his head counselor Bob Forrest look back on season five and then visit with Sean Young, Dwight Gooden, Jessica Kiper, and Steven Adler to see how they are coping out in the real world, a hundred and fifty days after discharge. Jessica struggles with a difficult, life changing decision, and Bob Forrest confronts Steven Adler at a concert," the program guide said.

Harris was pretty sure he'd be getting to know plenty of celebrities as manager of the East Hollywood Starbucks. He'd hand them their lattes, smile and say, "On me."

And no one would get more free lattes than Angie, whose money would be no good at all. He'd wink and say, "We're not taking any American Express Platinum cards today, Angie."

What he could not know is that, while Angie certainly enjoyed her soy Chai lattes, she detested the people who worked at Starbucks.

"They all want to be somebody, but they don't even know who they want to be," she told Tom. "They just want to be somebody different than they are."

Harris wanted to be somebody different. Anybody. He was making the changes he thought would allow him to pull it off. He was happy that evening, as happy as he'd been in a long time.

***

"I don't care about your bullshit legacy Tom," she told him that afternoon. "I don't care about your stupid books. None of that matters."

Things had been rough between them since his return from Nevada, even though he wasn't drinking. She was pissed at how he'd treated her on the San Francisco trip and that the first few days of his Nevada adventure had been nothing but a continuation of the bender he'd begun up north.

They were sitting in Il Capriccio on Vermont eating the lasagna and dipping the fresh baked bread into little bowls of a roasted garlic spiced olive oil that tasted faintly of anchovies and drinking glasses of sparkling Pellegrino water.

"I don't care about how many goddamn copies you sold or what they said about you in the *New York Times* four years ago or how many fat, middle-aged housewives show up when you give one of your stupid readings."

"What do you care about?" Tom asked.

"I care about someone who lives in the light instead of the darkness and I want someone who isn't afraid to actually show up for life," Angie said. "I've read the biographical stuff, I've talked to your friends. You're a broken down old drunk who's hurt a lot of people. And that kind of lifestyle doesn't interest me one bit."

65

"Who's your favorite poet?" Tom asked, seeming to change the subject.

"What?"

"Who's your favorite poet?"

"Poe?"

"Most Americans say that. And what's your favorite poem by him?"

"Annabelle Lee."

"Now, most people say 'The Raven,' but 'Annabelle Lee' is even better."

"Better for what?"

"Well, they're both about his wife, you know…"

"Of course."

"Who he married when he was twenty-seven and she was thirteen."

"I didn't know she was that young but…"

"Did you know that, during their marriage, he was fucking around with Frances Sargent Osgood and Elizabeth Ellett, who were like a couple of the top poetry groupies of the day…?"

"I never heard that."

"And that, while the poor girl was sick and dying of tuberculosis in a freezing cottage up in the Bronx, he was out with his buddies drinking enough bourbon and laudanum to kill a horse?"

"And your point is?" Angie said.

"When you think of Edgar Allen Poe, do you think of him as a broken down, womanizing drunk or as one of the two or three best poets America ever produced? Do you think of his poor wife or about 'Annabelle Lee?'"

"Fuck you Tom," she said. "Just… *Don't turn around.*"

"What?"

"Kiefer Sutherland just walked in the back door. He's with some tall blonde."

Tom started to say something but then Sutherland's voice

boomed from behind him.

"Angie!" Kiefer exclaimed.

She stood up and he came over to the table and hugged her. Tom didn't stand up. The tall blonde kept a respectable distance behind.

"Kiefer, this is Tom Heaton."

"The writer?" Sutherland said, smiling and offering his hand. He was only around five-nine and Tom was a little surprised. "Nice to meet you."

"Yeah," he said, shaking hands. "I've always admired your work."

"Tom's going into rehab on Monday," Angie chimed in.

"Well, we've all got our demons," Sutherland said. "Good luck Tom."

"Thanks, man."

"Anyway, I'm famished. How's the lasagna today?"

"To die for," Angie said.

"My table's waiting in back," he replied. "Great to see you Angie. Good to meet you Tom."

"Take care man," Tom said as Kiefer planted a peck on Angie's cheek.

"So how do you know Kiefer Sutherland?" Tom asked after he'd gone.

"His father and I were close back when I managed the Rainbow Room," she replied.

CHAPTER ELEVEN

The nail that sticks out gets hammered back in, they say in Florence, though neither Tom nor Angie had ever been to Florence and, even if they had been, they would have considered the saying an archaic adage of a backwards people. Because all they wanted to do was stick out. The way they dressed, the way they talked, the restaurants they ate at and even old Rowena herself all demanded attention. They lived in a place where celebrity was sought after as much as wealth, and the reason for someone's celebrity mattered less than the way the celebrities themselves managed and capitalized on it.

They both started young, Angie at fifteen years old on the Sunset Strip, where she'd once been picked up for prostitution, hanging out in glam venues like Rodney Bingenheimer's English Disco, dating older, well-known musicians, and having her picture taken for publications such as *Creem, Oui* and the short-lived and scandalous teen magazine *Star*, with its tawdry coverage of LA's underage groupie scene.

Around the same time, Tom was fronting a garage band in New York and writing for any newspaper or magazine that would print his byline. He played CBGB when it mattered and Max's Kansas City. He made a half dozen punk rock records that gave him cred years later in a way most writers could never know. Hunter Thompson and Johnny Thunders were his heroes and he began drinking, drugging and traveling as much as he could.

All of that had been ages ago, of course, with many husbands, wives, mistresses, lovers and dead friends chalked up since, like bugs on a windshield; scads of money squandered, piles of drugs, an ocean of booze and drama, high drama and more drama.

In short, they were pretty much the typical kind of fiftyish couple you might expect to meet on any given evening in Hollywood. The fight to be good people, against the lures of selfishness and conceit, was overwhelming for them.

They were nice people, Tom and Angie, just shallow.

***

"Eat my pussy," she hissed like a snake, lying on her back in the big bed she'd picked out for his apartment.

He'd been pounding her into the soft mattress for some time, traumatizing the bedframe so that it banged into the wall every time he lunged. She came and came again. He pulled out and slid down, licking and sucking and digging his nose in, kneading her breasts with his hands and she moaned and came again in a sweet gush that filled his mouth and slid down his throat.

"Oh my God," she said when he climbed back up on her. She was smiling and out of breath. Her cheeks were flushed. Her eyes were wild. "That was so fucking good, baby. I came three times."

"Now it's my turn," he said.

Then, from another room, he could hear the strains of the MC-5 doing "Kick Out the Jams."

"Shit," she said. "I was supposed to call Jamie this morning about that shoot on Tuesday. "Would you grab my phone? It's on the dining room table."

"Stay here," he said. "You're not done yet."

He got off the bed and pulled on a pair of jeans. He got her the phone and she started talking so he took a Lucky Strike out of the pack on his desk and went outside on the terrace to smoke. It was a beautiful warm spring day. The afternoon sun baked the painted wood planking of the deck and burned the soles of his feet. She talked and talked.

Finally, he heard her say, "OK Jamie, I'll see you there," and he went back in to find her fully clothed, wearing her sunglasses and pulling on her trademark Chanel boots.

"You're kidding right?" he said.

"Babe, I gotta go. They're doing the wardrobe fittings today."

"I didn't come."

"That's not my fault."

"Well, yeah, it kind of is."

"You know the problem with you Tom? You are so fucking selfish it's sickening. The whole world doesn't revolve around you, you know."

She picked up her purse and headed for the door.

"I can't even fucking believe this," he said.

"Call me later, because I won't call you," she replied, not looking back.

He watched her ass as she walked down to the courtyard, her boots echoing on the pavement, and then out to her Escalade. The horn sounded when she clicked the remote unlocking the doors and she got in and drove away.

***

The setting sun shone golden through the purple lavender trees and into the windows of the homes of the Silver Lake Hills, where American Craftsman style houses stood side by side with Spanish haciendas or fanciful Gothic castles, Frank Lloyd Wright inspired knockoffs and the nauseating poured concrete outrages attributable to the Modernists; each with its own dappled pool out back and happy or unhappy people inside drinking fruit juice or wine or gin and tonics, getting ready for dinner and pretending they were never going to die.

CHAPTER TWELVE

Meanwhile, over in Glendale, coarse Armenian gangsters hung around in front of a faux, Old World coffee house, doing their best to look like their Italian counterparts back east in New York and failing comically in their efforts.

The clothes were wrong, the shoes were wrong, the sunglasses were wrong and, most importantly, they were fucking Armenians, who were kind of like the Beverley Hillbillies of Europe. Most of them had come over in the 1990s, when the fact that they couldn't even get along with each other led to economic difficulties and bloody, full scale civil war.

Harris walked past them down the darkening outdoor mall after having had his hair cut by a fat Armenian stylist with big tits and a short skirt. He didn't really know what to ask for, at the barber shop he usually went to he'd say, "a regular" and they'd know what he meant. His hair hadn't been long enough to do anything with in the first place and so the stylist gave him a buzz cut like she did with all the Armenian men of his age. When he saw himself in the mirror he was a little taken aback. He'd been hoping for more of a Johnny Depp kind of thing, but it would have to do. On the way back to his apartment, he stopped off at the drugstore and bought a pair of twenty-dollar aviator sunglasses – which was what the Armenian gangsters wore – and they mitigated things somewhat.

He stopped for a beer at a big, airy sports bar he happened to be passing. There were no games of interest on any of the fourteen wide-screen television sets around the place, nor were there any customers. While he waited for a bartender, or a waitress, or anyone to come and serve him, he called up Cookie. He wanted to try out his new ensemble and figured Tony would only make fun of it down at the Drawing Room.

"What the hell do you want?" Cookie said, answering the phone.

"I thought you might like to go out tonight Cookie. I was..."

"Are you fucking kidding me? You fired me from my job. I lost three-and-a-half credits at school and now I'm not going to graduate, you asshole."

"C'mon baby..."

"And anyway," she said. "What makes you think I don't already have a date on a Saturday night?"

"Do you?"

"I would rather watch the hairs on my legs grow than go out with you again, asshole."

"Hang on a sec," Harris said as a guy appeared behind the bar. "Lemme have an Atwater Brotherhood Ale," he told him.

"Hon, I didn't know they were going to take those credits away. C'mon, let me make it up to you. *The Avengers* is playing at the Pacific..."

But Cookie had already hung up.

"Let me get a double Black Velvet with that too," he told the barman when he came back with the beer.

Later he had a couple more beers at home before putting on his new outfit and heading over to the Drawing Room. Tony was there alone, as usual, staring at his own reflection in the mirror behind the bar.

"Who the hell are you supposed to be?" he asked, when he saw Harris.

"Fuck you, Tony," Harris replied.

They sat together for the rest of the night, Tony talking about all the chicks who would come to see his band at the Silver Lake Farmer's Market and Harris speaking in solemn tones about his future career at Starbucks. Each of them might just as well have been sitting alone in a room, talking to themselves.

Somebody played the Eagles on the jukebox, "Peaceful Easy Feeling," and Harris was reminded again of just how much he hated the Eagles.

***

The problem for Angie was that she really had fallen in love with Tom. It was strange to her, bizarre almost. It had been a long time since she'd felt anything more than friendship for any guy. Now all of a sudden she found herself saying things like "I'm seeing someone," or "My boyfriend's from New York" in order to discourage would-be suitors.

She loved his gravelly voice and she loved the way he'd rub her back and her legs until she fell asleep on the couch while they watched television, her head sliding down on his belly like it was a pillow.

Now she slept more easily beside him than she did by herself.

The feelings confused her and she rebelled against them, telling him never to call her again or that it was over between them, but then he'd take her out to dinner at one of the neighborhood places they liked and she would fall in love with him all over again.

God damn it. How had she become such a pushover? Angie wondered. How had her whole life changed so drastically in such a short time? Before Tom came, ten guys a day would call to ask her out or chat her up. Now when the phone rang, she knew it was him or her mother or her sister or work.

She'd read his old stories, about women he'd been in love with ten or twenty or even thirty years ago, and get mad and jealous. She looked at the pictures of him from back then, from old rock magazines or on the dust jackets of his books, and think how unfair it was that she got him when he was an old broken down drunk instead of the dashing figure he sometimes presented himself as when he was a young man.

But even still she loved him. And although she'd wanted to fall in love for so bad so long, now that she had she wasn't sure she liked it. She wondered where it would all end.

Three of Angie's four previous husbands had been addicts, but Tom was her first drunk. *"Goddammit,"* she told herself. *"You said you were never gonna do this again. At least junkies can get clean. Drunks are always drunks."*

"FUCK YOU!" she screamed at an elderly Filipina driving a beat up Mercedes 300 series. The woman had changed lanes unexpectedly in front of her. "ASSHOLE!"

Now she was in too deep and she knew it. It had been nearly ten years since she let anyone inside her, *really* inside her, and now she'd let him and now – even when she'd made up her mind, made the irrevocable decision, washed that man right out of her hair – he could show up at her door, a paper sack of those salted, dark chocolate covered almonds in hand, wearing his goddamn black suit and fancy boots, hair all slicked back, shades, and goddamn him, goddamn him GODDAMN HIM!

At the corner of Hillhurst, she stopped as two young blondes in running gear sprinted through the crosswalk in front of her.

"You can't run away from ugly," she shouted at them.

By nighttime she'd be sitting in his beat old Cadillac, necking with him, making out, talking when he'd let her get a word in edgewise, holding out on fucking him right there just because she thought she should.

Old Rowena would sit in the backseat, complaining when the conversation began to drag on a little bit too long. On the Nevada trip, the dog had gotten used to sitting next to Tom in the front seat, and now she just wanted to go home and to bed.

Tom put his lips to Angie's and his fingers into her long black hair and he felt her skull and stuck his tongue into her mouth. He so loved her. She was the Queen of Heaven, the most beautiful girl in Hollywood.

She had an early call the next morning and decided to stay at her place for the night. It was hard for her to do but she felt she had to maintain some semblance of her own identity, some reminder of her essential self. She could stop by his apartment on the way to work and they'd go for coffee. Before she went to bed, she sent him an email.

"i love you baby... tonight was great.... see you in the morning......xox," it said.

When he got home and read it, he felt as good as he ever had.

CHAPTER THIRTEEN

While he waited, Harris stared at the sign they'd placed him in front of.

"Starbucks Shared Planet," it read.

"You and Starbucks. It's bigger than coffee."

Way bigger, Harris thought looking around. They had twenty different kinds of pastries. And breakfast sandwiches and lunch sandwiches and the various teas and lemonades and everything else. But even he realized that mostly what they sold was cool, a brand of corporate cool akin to the Target chain selling Ramones T shirts now that Joey and Johnny and Dee Dee were dead.

"It's our commitment to doing business in ways that are good to the earth and to each other. From the way we buy our COFFEE, to minimizing our environmental footprint, to being involved in local COMMUNITIES. It's doing things the way we always have. And using our size for good. And because you support us, Starbucks Shared Planet is what YOU are a part of too."

Just drinking coffee at Starbucks made you a part of something bigger and better than anything you might be now or could even ever imagine being. He thought of Angie rather than Josef Goebbels, who could have written the ill-punctuated and grammatically challenged screed himself, but Harris quite naturally had no idea who Josef Goebbels was.

So instead he thought of Angie and the sheer profundity of

it all. He was about to change his whole life for her, a life long misbegotten, he realized now, a life that wasn't really a life at all. He hadn't even been living.

All that business about good and evil, about life being without purpose and how free will didn't exist, how had he let himself believe that bullshit? How could he let himself sink so low?

Now he would enter a larger universe where even something as insignificant as getting a cup of coffee created an impact felt all around the world. Where a woman like Angie could be comfortable and wear designer clothes and affect the future of the entire planet in a positive way all at the same time. No sacrifice was too great.

***

She told him she'd be over at four but she wasn't. Tom was used to it. In all the time he'd known her she was never once within an hour of a time she'd set for herself. At six o'clock she called and said she was on her way and at six thirty called again to say that something had come up.

She thought that this selfish, inconsiderate and ultimately boorish sort of behavior constituted some sort of charming eccentricity, to the extent that she often told what she believed were amusing anecdotes about it. They usually ended with her saying, "When I showed up late for my wedding they said, 'Angie, you'll be late for your own funeral!'"

And it never, ever, ever even crossed her mind that the people she constantly stood up, kept waiting, put on ice and left cooling their heels found it to be about the most annoying thing on the fucking face of the planet. And even if she had realized it, she wouldn't have cared at all. Because it was never about anybody else. It was always about Angie.

If he said anything about it, she would begin to scream and

accuse him of trying to "keep tabs" on her.

He knew he would see her again eventually and that, when he did, the first thing she would tell him would be either that she was exhausted or she was really hungry.

It wouldn't have mattered. He was used to it and put up with it because he loved her, but the next day he was supposed to go into rehab and there was no telling how long it would be until they were really alone together again.

"I'm walking out to the car now," she told him when he called again. But he knew she was lying.

Both of them were enormously adept liars, and they lied to each other all the time. They were the worst kind of liars. They even believed their own lies.

***

"How you doing man?"

The kid came up behind him and Harris was startled.

"Hey," he managed.

The kid seemed much younger than him even though he wasn't and was wearing a black T-shirt and jeans. His tousled hair and three-day growth of youthful beard gave the impression of casual informality Harris recognized but had never been able to achieve. If not for the fact that he had Harris's resume and other paperwork in his hand, Harris would have thought he was simply one of the rockers or industry guys for whom the East Hollywood Starbucks was a second home. Instead he was the district manager.

They shook hands.

"It's such a beautiful afternoon, why don't we take this outside," the kid said brightly. "I'm Don Kaiser."

"Uh, sure," Harris stuttered.

"Would you like something to drink?"

"Coffee. Black, please."

Dammit! I meant to order Chai latte soy, seven pumps, no water and lots of extra foam, Harris thought. Already he was screwing things up.

Don went to the counter and ordered Harris's coffee along with an ice cold Tazo Green Tea Frappuccino™ for himself.

Don got the drinks and motioned Harris outside. It was eighty eight degrees and they sat on the black stamped sheet metal chairs at one of the sunbaked black metal tables. The tables were so hot you could have cooked beans on them unless you got one of the few covered by the green canvas, Starbucks logoed umbrellas. Which were for paying customers.

"Let me ask you something," Don said then. "I see that most of your background and experience is in the fast food hamburger business. What makes you think you want to work at Starbucks?"

"Well, Mr. Kaiser..." Harris began.

"Don," Don said. "We like to keep things on a first name basis here at Starbucks, Bob."

"John," Harris said.

"What?"

"John. My Christian name is John."

"Whatever," Don smiled. "I mean, why not just move into one of the more upscale burger chains? Carl's Jr., In-N-Out, they're all hiring right now, Bob."

Harris's feet were starting to itch in his cheap boots and he could feel the sweat that was pouring down his forehead. There wasn't a cloud in the sky and the sweltering sun beat down mercilessly. The black polyester blend sport coat was hot to the touch and so were the black jeans. He thought that if he sat there like that another minute he might spontaneously combust.

"I'm through with burgers Mr., I mean Don," Harris stuttered. "I want to be a part of something bigger, I want to be a part of something, you know, something *important.*"

Through a plastic straw and from a plastic container that

wouldn't biodegrade under normal landfill conditions for ten thousand years, Don sipped his Tazo Green Tea Frappuccino™. One day, archeologists in hazmat suits, excavating what is now the Santa Monica Bay but will by that time be just another overbuilt suburb, a part of the vast urban sprawl that is greater Los Angeles, will come across that particular plastic container and straw, cataloguing it and having no idea of its significance to Harris's life on this hot afternoon at the intersection where Vermont meets Hollywood and Sunset.

"You do realize, don't you, that our customers are fundamentally different than those you would normally encounter at Jack in the Box, no?"

"Totally," Harris said. He was elated. Don had given him just the opening he needed to rattle off the demographic data he'd picked up on the internet.

"I don't have to tell you, Don, that it all gets down to customer service," he wrapped up. "And even though Starbucks charges more than McDonald's and 7-11, I think we both know the people who come here are willing to pay more for the good customer service that justifies the extra costs and makes them feel valued."

"Very good," Don said. "See Bob, the people who work at the company and the seventy million people a week who support us know we are consistently embracing values in the way we practice business. You know, Starbucks has always tried to manage its business by balancing profitability with a social conscience, and that has served us well. If you look at the history of companies 'doing the right thing,' you'll see that most have performed extremely well."

Confident now, Harris reached out and picked up his coffee.

"It's all about values, Don," he nodded.

"I see here that you want to work at this particular Starbucks location," Don said. "That's really kind of unusual.

Why this store?"

Again, Harris was prepared. He couldn't say anything about Angie, of course, about the momentous, life changing effect she had on him, or of his plans, not yet fully formed, to win her heart.

"I just see a lot of potential... I come here quite a lot and I've noticed that the baristas often get the orders wrong. Also, they take the outdoor chairs and tables in at ten o'clock when the restaurant stays open till midnight. It's those little touches, I think, that keep this location from being all that it can be, revenue-wise, Don."

"Wow," Don said. "You've really done your homework. That's great."

Harris remembered, for a fleeting moment, Angie's discarded piece of blueberry scone. His shirt collar was soaking. The sweat was stinging his eyes. He tried to maintain his composure.

"I put a lot of thought into this," he said, blinking. "I'd like to put my management experience to work here and do what I've been able to do at the Jack in the Box on Colorado Street."

"That's great, man... The only other thing, I see here you were in the Army."

With the buzz cut that Armenian woman had given him, Harris looked like he was still in the Army.

"Awhile ago. Is that a problem?"

"No, no, not at all. In fact, thanks for your service, you know? Where did they have you?"

"Iraq," Harris said. "Afghanistan."

"Wow. Bad scene. You ever kill anybody?"

They all asked that. All the civilians. He was in Hollywood, where they made movies the civilians watched thinking that's what war was like. But they had no fucking clue. No idea. They took their paychecks and saw what had been deducted for the federal income tax and thought it was going to provide for the poor. Or something.

"Yes Don," he said. "As a matter of fact I have... killed somebody."

He looked directly at Don, waiting for a response. It was funny. They all asked you that and, when you told them, they never had any response. They didn't even know what they were culpable for.

Instead Don explained that there were no management spots open, no assistant manager positions or even team leader opportunities. Harris would have to start from the bottom, as a humble barista. The pay was eight twenty five an hour and, based on a thirty five hour workweek, Harris could count on taking home something under three hundred dollars every payday, less than half what he made at Jack in the Box.

It was a disappointment, to be sure. In his mind he juggled some numbers, how much he had in the bank, the money he could save by not going out so much and how quickly he would begin climbing the Starbucks corporate ladder. Plus there were the tips, he thought.

"When do I start?" he asked.

***

They sat *al fresco* at the Desert Rose, a charming Hollywood café on Hillhurst where they knew the owner and the waitresses all looked like models in the Victoria's Secret catalogues. They'd been fighting.

About what it didn't matter. They were always fighting now, and Tom found himself looking at condos in Vegas and good-sized sailboats moored at Marina Del Ray on Craigslist.

She was complaining about money and saying that, since he'd moved out there, she was no longer working enough. It was his fault.

"I have a life," she told him. "I can't be with you every

second of every day."

He started to tell her he didn't want every second of every day, only a couple or three hours, but she cut him off.

"I'm not through," she scolded.

In just the past six months he'd dropped well over ninety grand on her, paying her car bills and her plumbing bills and the veterinary bills racked up by the Maltese puppy she'd insisted he buy her even though the poor thing was near death and had to be put on intravenous life support immediately. He bought her jewelry and clothes and took her out every day and night to restaurants she liked.

And now she was saying how she was broke and had to start working more in order to make ends meet. It would mean seeing him less of course, but he was just going to have to learn how to sit home alone and wait while she slaved away having to look all beautiful and sexy and ready to go in some dumbass music video, and not be troubled the next day, when the photos of her locked in warm embrace with whoever the lead singer was were plastered all over the internet gossip sites.

Going away to rehab for a month became less and less appealing to him by the second.

"You remember the Chambers Brothers, don't you? Anyway, the guy actually wrote the song about me. It's a two day shoot out by Joshua Tree next week," she sparkled. "I've got the tape. We'll listen to it when we get home. He uses a different name than mine because he's married, but it's about me."

He said nothing. He looked at his watch. He drummed his fingers on the white linen tablecloth.

The night was beautiful and warm and they sat at a small table underneath strings of sparkling white lights the affable Armenian owner had strung over the courtyard. Tom ate a filet mignon, medium well, as did Rowena, who sat ladylike on his lap and never begged. Angie ate a grilled chicken kabob with a side of tabbouleh and they both drank sparkling Pellegrino water with lime. The whole thing would set him back eighty bucks with the tip, and he wished he could have at least had a glass of Johnny Walker for that kind of dough.

CHAPTER FOURTEEN

He loved her. What could he do? In the end she was right. He was a broken down drunk who'd hurt a lot of people and had a lot to be sorry about. He'd ruined his looks with booze and drugs and fistfights and car wrecks, he had a bum knee and a weak liver that was like a ticking time bomb inside of him. Over the years people had used various psychiatric phrases like bipolar and even sociopathic to describe him more times than he could remember. He drove himself out to Pasadena and pulled into the parking lot of the Casa de las Encina, an upscale but unostentatious rehab center they had there.

The grassy campus was shaded by beautiful trees of every description and the architecture was of the old Mission style with lots of dark wood and stained glass and wooden chairs and benches that looked pretty but were uncomfortable to sit on. As he got out of the Cadillac he noticed several cats walking or napping on the lawn.

Tom knew the drill. He'd been there before.

Not a place so nice, of course, and, the last time, he hadn't driven in himself but had gone in an ambulance. An acute case of alcohol poisoning combined with a reported suicide attempt. During the bad time after his daughter died.

He hadn't meant to hang himself but only to upset Rachel, who was in the other room flirting with a newspaper acquaintance who'd stopped by for cocktails. Tom had been drinking all day and was in no mood for drama.

In any event, they put him in an ambulance and took him out to Queens where he was confined to a lockdown ward full of other would-be suicides and detoxing heroin addicts and simple criminals for whom detox and rehab were part of their court sentences.

He'd see the lady psychologist in the morning and eat the hospital food three times a day and read while the other inmates watched cartoons on television. At night before bed somebody from Alcoholics Anonymous or Narcotics Anonymous would come in and give an inspirational talk. Rachel came and brought him cigarettes and quarters for the phone and the vending machines and he made small gifts to some of those who had been sentenced and everybody pretty much left him alone.

For Tom, the high point of his five-day detox and observation stay came on the last night when he got out of bed and went to the break room for a smoke. A crack addict named Vicki came in and didn't have a light so he gave her one and one thing led to another and he fucked her from behind as she bent over a heavy old wooden table.

***

The Demon Star Algol – one of the fifteen malevolent Behenian stars of Thoth manifesting itself on earth through a poisonous variety of black hellebore plant and the gemstones we know as diamonds -- flickers and dims in the vast universe, providing the blinking eye of the snake-headed Gorgon Medusa in the constellation of Perseus. To the Chinese it is known as the Fifth Star of the Mausoleum, the *Tseih She,* or Pile of Corpses.

Considered the most unfortunate star in the heavens by astrologers and associated with bloody violence across a wide variety of cultures, it was getting ready to go retrograde in Taurus, which was Harris's own birth sign.

As with so many things, Harris was completely unaware of what was about to happen ninety-three light years away from his shabby Glendale apartment, ignorant even of the existence of Algol or what it represented. He only knew he had a headache, and that it wasn't getting any better.

Rehab. He'd been hanging around with drunks and dope fiends ever since he was a little kid. He felt right at home.

There was the usual assortment of rich white kids with meth habits whose parents had gone to Europe and didn't want to come back to a wrecked and looted home, and Phil Lynott's old songwriting partner Jimmy Bain, who was there on a grant from the Grammy Foundation following a possession for distribution bust and knew Tom from the old days; the striking and statuesque daughter of a famous Mexican movie star talking in Spanish to a cartel driver from Long Beach who'd made his living ferrying stolen Mercedes and BMWs across the border at TJ, returning a few hours later in some beat to shit Honda packed with cocaine; a commercial real estate developer hooked on Vicodin and the former manager of the largest Porsche dealership in Beverly Hills, there to lose his heroin habit. A leggy twenty-four-year-old looker hugging a teddy bear and sucking her thumb.

Here the dysfunctional and addled took a vacation from their habits, from themselves, living and acting more normally than they had in ages. For some, the experience would be enough to get them to kick whatever it was they craved, but for most the stay would constitute but a brief holiday, a thirty or sixty or ninety-day respite from the serious work and business of getting high.

"I mean, I'm like what's the point where you call 911?" he heard a pretty young blonde say as she crossed the lobby to the elevator. "When they turn blue or what?"

You could get the monkey off your back, Tom thought, but the circus was always in town.

***

Like Harris, Tom and Angie saw not what awaited them. They knew only that the miscommunication, incessant bickering and sniping between the two of them was escalating, and that good days often turned to bad for no apparent reason.

In Miami, a man was shot to death by police after pouncing on a naked, homeless guy sleeping under a bridge and *eating his face*. Police likened the attack to one by a zombie, and said that when they ordered the cannibal to stop, he looked up and growled at them.

Near Monterrey Mexico, the mutilated bodies of forty nine men and women were dumped near the entrance to the peaceful village of San Juan, each with its head, hands and feet hacked off by a chainsaw. Police said the victims had likely been slaughtered elsewhere two days earlier and brought to San Juan in the back of a dump truck.

A world away, in the Tibetan capital of Lhasa, a dozen Buddhist monks doused themselves with kerosene and set themselves ablaze in the public square, and in the Houla region of Syria, near the Biblical city of Bethel, one hundred and eight mostly women and children were shot and stabbed to death as they rose from their midmorning prayers.

An international manhunt was underway for the "Canadian Psycho" Luka Magnotta, a preternaturally attractive twenty-nine-year-old porn star who killed and dismembered his gay lover in their Montreal apartment, videotaping the atrocity and posting it on the internet before sending severed body parts to Canadian politicians and various media outlets. Cops in LA were investigating Magnotta in connection with the murder and dismemberment of a guy named Hervey Medellin, whose decapitated body was discovered under the iconic Hollywood sign a few months earlier.

Even the heated American presidential election campaign seemed irrelevant in light of these outrages but that night, that very night, 21.5 million people in the United States would tune into an updated version of the old Ted Mack Amateur Hour program called "American Idol," in which previously anonymous middle American contestants sang their hearts out in hope of winning a record contract. Another 34.6 million would watch one of two episodes of a show called "Dancing With the Stars," in which professional dancers were paired with often clumsy D-List celebrities in a hokey competition that seemed designed as much to humiliate the contestants as to uncover any innate and heretofore undiscovered rhythmic ability.

Americans just didn't give a shit. And that was the way Hollywood liked it.

***

Tom laughed out loud. Angie would have loved this, he thought. Maybe he'd call her.

"They're kidding, right?" he said to the guy standing next to him in the hallway.

"Tonight's Speaker: Heidi Fleiss," the sign read.

"Somehow, I don't think so," the guy said. He wasn't laughing. "Two weeks ago they had Rodney King."

Heidi Fleiss was a Hollywood hooker turned madam best known for her thousand-dollar blowjobs prior to a 1993 arrest on pandering and tax evasion charges. The case made national news because her client list included many famous and wealthy show business types, but she kept her mouth shut and parlayed the whole thing into a documentary film, a made for TV movie and a ghostwritten memoir that turned her into a minor league celebrity herself.

In the twenty years that had passed, she appeared sporadically on the *FOX News Network* as a guest commentator, wrote a column for *Maxim*, was arrested for drug possession and impaired driving, starred in season three of "Celebrity

Rehab" and ended up running a laundromat in Pahrump, Nevada, near Death Valley, where she lived with twenty-nine parrots she inherited from a dead friend.

And now, Tom discovered, she was also moonlighting as a motivational speaker. He liked dried up, diseased old whores as much as the next guy but there just seemed something odd about it. The thought that being a sort of famous lowlife qualified someone to hand out advice about substance abuse or anything else was somehow disturbing.

And when the time came, it was every bit as bad as he thought it would be. Wide eyed and wired, with teeth as big as last year's Kentucky Derby winner, Fleiss looked easily a decade older than her forty-five years.

"I'm Heidi Fleiss and I was the greatest madam that ever lived," she began. "Every woman's a hooker to me. When someone calls me a whore, I think it's a compliment. I took the oldest profession on earth and I did it better than anyone on earth. Alexander the Great conquered the world at thirty-two. I conquered it at twenty-two."

Tom was motivated all right. He was motivated to get the hell out of there and find a bar so he could have a drink like a normal person.

"I had a bit of a substance abuse problem," Heidi continued. "If I wanted my Vicodin I was going to take my Vicodin. And if I want a little of that Crystal Meth... Rush Limbaugh was my idol, though. He was taking thirty OxyContin a day and doing that radio show..."

She rambled on and on. Soon, audience members were talking to each other in hushed tones. Why are we listening to this? What the hell was she on? Rodney King had been more articulate than she was.

"When I was a madam and running my illegal business, drugs were just kind of like party favors... I am sober right now but, after the penitentiary I had low self-esteem or, I don't know what, something made me start to do drugs again… I have a drug problem but I just can't be lonely any more…."

For the love of Christ, Tom thought. *Would somebody help this poor woman?*

"I would love to meet a guy, I would love a man in my life," she said. "But really, I'm all about the money."

Finally she'd said something that made sense, Tom thought. Because every woman in Hollywood was all about the money. And no matter how much money you had, they'd tell you they could always get someone who had more.

***

"I'm surprised you called," Joel said.

They were sitting in Flore, a filthy vegan restaurant on Sunset in the filthiest part of Silver Lake. Tom was in rehab but, even if he wasn't, Angie knew he would never go there. Not in a million years. It was the sort of scene he had spent much of his life trying to avoid. The place was crawling with hipsters.

"I just don't know what I'm going to do," she said.

"I've always been your friend, Angie," he said, reaching across the grimy two-spot and touching her hand. "I've always been here for you and you know that."

"Tom's gone into rehab," she said.

"He ought to be in a zoo," Joel said. The spot near his temple where the blows had landed still felt tender.

The cooking scum covering the windows diffused the bright spring light coming in from outside. Beneath their feet, the floor stuck to the soles of their shoes.

"I don't know what I'm going to do, Joel," she said.

Just then, the gay waiter, who was actually (surprise!) an aspiring actor, brought them the acai berry smoothies they'd ordered and set them down on the table with a flourish.

She wasn't going to bang Joel. It hadn't even crossed her

mind. But she was pissed at Tom, pissed because he was a drunk and because he'd been bitching lately about money, but pissed mostly because he'd made her fall madlessly in love with him and there was nothing she could do about it.

"Everybody always said we looked so good together Angie," Joel said. "We used to have a lot of fun."

***

Harris phoned the district office bright and early Monday morning to make sure they'd received his two-week notice, which he'd faxed from Copy Central on North Brand near his apartment in Glendale about a half hour earlier. The girl put him on hold to wait for Sean Neiderlander, a punk kid with a business degree who held the title of Harris's immediate supervisor.

The hold music, Kenny G, was way too loud, and he held the cell away from his ear.

"Yes Harris, this is Sean Neiderlander," Neiderlander said finally.

"Hi, Mr. Neiderlander," Harris said, not realizing he could have said, "Hey shithead," and there wouldn't have been anything Neiderlander could do about it. "I was just wondering if you'd gotten my two-week notice."

"Yes Harris, I have it right here."

There was an awkward pause.

"Well, I've been working here for quite awhile, and I thought it was only right I give the company two weeks to try to find someone to replace me."

"Are you in the store now?"

"Yes sir. Ten a.m. on the dot."

"Right," Neiderlander said. "Let's see. And you're scheduled for Wednesday, right?"

"Wednesday, right. I told them at..."

Neiderlander cut him off.

"There's really no reason for you to come in on Wednesday, Harris. No reason at all," he said. "What we'll do is have somebody drop around this afternoon and collect your keys, bring the severance papers around for you to sign, and I'm sure that Jack in the Box appreciates all you've done."

He watched Joachim, the assistant manager, shoot him a sideways glance from over near the produce bins.

"It's just that I've had this amazing opportunity and I feel that, for my own growth, I need to..." Harris realized then that Neiderlander had already hung up.

"You have a good day, Mr. Neiderlander," he said loudly, staring at Joachim all the while. "And good luck to you too, sir."

And Harris didn't know, didn't know until that very day, that it was Joachim all along. Later that afternoon, before they came to get the keys and have him sign the severance papers, Harris fired his underling, still thinking that anything he could do would make any difference whatsoever on the face of the whole fucking planet.

CHAPTER FIFTEEN

Angie lay on the couch in her pajamas playing with the sick little Maltese, letting it bite her on the face and pull her hair. The puppy was so little and helpless and she loved it so much.

It was the first really relaxing night she'd had in weeks. Honestly, she was glad Tom had gone away. He was so fucking intense she couldn't stand it sometimes.

"Who's Mommy's baby girl?" she said to the puppy.

She really needed to dye her hair. She hadn't touched up her roots since before she and Tom started arguing, before they went to San Francisco, before he took off to Nevada, before she started noticing that she'd given over so much of her life to him that there wasn't much left for her anymore.

It was like he wanted to be with her every second of every day. He was even jealous of the hours she spent sleeping.

It had gotten so that she felt she was walking on eggshells all the time, afraid of his anger and sadness when someone would call and take her away from him. She didn't realize that what she thought of as pressure, him saying he missed her, that he wanted to see her and how he wished he could spend more time with her, would have been thought of by him as compliments, treasures, had she said those words to him.

But she never said them, and the puppy bit her on the eyelid, which would give her a black eye that everyone would think Tom was responsible for in light of the fact that she'd told them all she was afraid of him. He'd have no more hit her than hit his own mother, of course, and she knew that.

The phone rang again and she saw his number and let it go straight to voicemail.

***

94

Tom escaped from rehab on the third night. It wasn't much of an escape as those things go; he simply packed the big gym bag he'd brought and walked down to the reception area.

"I'm outta here," he said to the guy sitting behind the big desk. "Send me the paperwork."

"You're not supposed to…" the guy began.

"I miss my dog," Tom said, letting the heavy wooden door swing shut behind him. "Good night."

He drove down the road and checked into the Langham, which was the only hotel he knew in Pasadena. His publisher had put him up there when he was doing the book tour.

After dropping his bag off in the room, he went back downstairs to the Tap Room. The cool night air came in off the terrace where bougainvillea in three colors swayed in the gentle breeze.

"What can I get you?" the bartender asked.

"Double Glenlivet on the rocks," he said. "I'm having a relapse."

"I get that all the time," the bartender said. There were a lot of rehabs in Pasadena.

Angie would be pissed but he didn't care. He thought of Merida, on the Yucatan peninsula, and the lush green of the jungle and the brown faces of the people in the streets. He thought how nice it always was to be in a place where nobody spoke English. Where you could go to a bullfight or bribe a policeman.

His life had been resonant with doubt and sadness, and he felt himself drifting in a transient, idle world like a character in some 17th Century Japanese novel.

"Living only for the moment, savoring the moon, the snow, the cherry blossoms and the maple leaves, singing songs, loving sake, women and poetry, letting oneself drift, buoyant and carefree, like a gourd carried along with the river current," the ukiyo novelist Asai Ryoi had written in 1661.

The bartender brought his whiskey and Tom handed him a twenty.

"Keep 'em coming," he said, turning on the barstool to look around the room.

He was the only man in the joint not wearing a tie. The place reeked of old money, and the people having their nightcaps or drinking more seriously were all dressed to the nines. There was one unattached woman, younger, beautiful like a fast piece of furniture and sitting down at the end of the bar. He sent over a drink when the bartender brought his and she came and joined him. She had those clear braces on her teeth, and it kind of turned him on.

They talked for fifteen minutes maybe, he told her who he was and that he'd just ditched rehab, and she told him she was trying to be a model. He found himself becoming annoyed by her constant fiddling with her iPhone.

It seemed to him that younger people had the attention spans of gnats, and he thought about a world where no one could understand a thought that took more than one hundred and forty characters to express.

He decided he hated Pasadena, and turned back on his barstool. The girl said it was nice to meet him. He had just ordered another drink when his phone rang. It was Angie. He had called her twenty times that day and now, after midnight, she was calling him back.

"Hey baby," he said.

"I miss you," she told him.

***

Harris woke up in a cold sweat. The pillowcase was drenched and the sheets stuck to his skin. Even the mattress was soaked and he wondered for a moment whether or not he'd pissed himself. His head felt like it was about to split open and it took him a minute to realize where he was. He reached over to the nightstand for his medication. His heart was pounding.

It was a nightmare. He dreamt that he'd finally started the new job at Starbucks but things got worse and worse. There was a line that went out the door and each person who came to the counter was talking on their iPhone, not giving their order, ignoring him. Then he saw Angie's mutt Chihuahua running around the store as he tried in vain to get the people to line up along the pastry case instead of straight back out the door. The dog growled at him and when he reached down to pet it snapped at him, and only by jerking his hand back quickly was he not bitten.

Finally he heard her voice from the back of the store, in amongst the crush of people, yelling.

"WHAT IS THE FUCKING PROBLEM HERE?" she cried. "ROWENA? C'MON GIRL... WHERE'S MY FUCKING DOG?"

Just then, the dog bit him on the ankle and his new black pants became saturated with blood. He grabbed the animal and put it under his arm, pushing people away and charging back to the sound of Angie's voice.

When he reached her, panicked and out of breath, she turned to him and looked up.

"It's pronounced venti, not VENTAY. And it's grande, not grand. And no, tall is not the biggest one. I didn't make up the goddamn rules, asshole," she said.

Harris plodded barefoot into the kitchen and took a can of Diet Coke out of the refrigerator. He sat down at the little Formica table in his boxer shorts and T-shirt, opened it and washed down the pills. It wasn't just the headache though. His earlobe throbbed from the piercing he'd had done that afternoon. He pulled at it with his fingers. He was miserable.

Scared.

Infected.

Tomorrow was his first day.

***

Angie wasn't mad that Tom left rehab, she'd known Heidi Fleiss and they laughed about that, but she was mad he was sitting in a hotel bar drinking. After she hung up on him he went back up to his room and got his bag, still unpacked on the bed, and left the hotel. He had to see her. He was addicted to her way more than he was addicted to the booze. It only took him twenty-five minutes to get back into Los Angeles but the Los Feliz and Glendale exit ramps were closed for nighttime construction and he overshot the neighborhood completely, getting off someplace in Burbank and becoming lost.

He walked up to her house in the blue predawn light and knocked on her door.

"Who is it?"

"Me."

She answered the door emerald eyes sleepy, wearing the same grey jeggings and sheer, oversized T-shirt she'd been wearing, sleeping in, when he saw her last. God, she was beautiful, he thought. Magnificent.

She let him in and put on some water for tea.

"You know, it finally dawned on me," he said, taking a banana off the kitchen table and peeling it.

"What?"

"All my life I've been going with skanks and whores. Now I've got a real lady and sometimes I don't know how to act."

"I want that in your damn book," she said and he laughed.

"I'm serious. You put that in your book."

They hugged and kissed and she took him by the hand and led him into her bedroom, and they lay down on top of her bed, him holding her and kissing the nape of her neck until she fell asleep. He was wide awake and just held her like that until the sun came streaming in through the windows and she woke up for real.

Her phone was ringing. It was Gretchen.

"Did you see this shit about Tom on Twitter?" she asked.

"No. What?"

"You better check it out. A girl I know, a lingerie model. Her name's Melissa Totten."

"Let me call you back," Angie said.

The tweets were brutal.

"No thanks, Tom, the writer/alcoholic sitting next to me talking about his screenplay for Kurt Russell and his escape from rehab LA earlier tonight"

"Tom is now talking about how he is an artist and believes everything happens for a reason, like how we've been brought together at this hotel" she wrote a few minutes later.

With the third tweet, there was a picture of Tom, wearing the same clothes he had on when he knocked on Angie's door a few hours earlier. He was smiling. Leering lecherously, Angie would say.

"Apparently Tom is a straightforward guy from New York who got a job at a newspaper when he was 19 and then fate and his own unstoppable talent took over from there"

It got worse and worse.

"He asked what I do for a living. I said model. He said "Oh I love meeting other artists like myself"

YOU MOTHERFUCKER! Angie screamed.

***

Back in New York it was three hours later, and Rachel awoke to the sound of the door buzzer.

"I'm coming," she said, getting up and pulling on her robe. On the nightstand, a half full bottle of coconut rum sat waiting.

The buzzer rang again. She swore and went and saw it was the mailman.

"Signature required," he said when she opened the door.

She didn't have her reading glasses on and squinted to see what it was or who it was from but it did her no good. She took the pen and scribbled her name on the paper he held out. He handed her the envelope, along with some others she didn't have to sign for.

"Thank you," she said.

She dropped the mail on the dining room table and turned on the coffee and fed the cats. She found her glasses and brought the rum out of her bedroom and, when the coffee was done, she fixed herself a royale.

Sitting down at the table, she picked up the envelope, which she now saw had come from the Los Angeles County Superior Court. She opened it to find Tom had filed for divorce.

"The motherfucker!" she said, slamming her hand on the table. Her eyes welled with tears and she began to cry.

She'd saved his goddamn life, got him back on his feet again and stood by his sorry ass through thick and thin for more than a dozen years. She'd typed and retyped the manuscript of his second book, edited and copy-edited and, once the revisions were done, called in publishing world chits and managed the job of book-selling for him. She'd even introduced him to Hank, who would become his agent.

She was so proud of him. *And now that he finally makes it, he dumps me for some botoxed Hollywood fame whore?* She couldn't even go on fucking Facebook without seeing a picture of the two of them together at some party or nightclub. Smiling. Having a great old time. It just wasn't fucking fair.

She drank the rummed up coffee and had another. She went in, took a shower, got dressed and put on some makeup. She looked up Vinnie DiCienzo's number in her phone and called it.

Vinnie was their attorney.

CHAPTER SIXTEEN

It took Tom two days to make it up with Angie. Once *TMZ* made it an item, the Totten woman's Twitter account grew to more than thirty-five thousand followers. The bitch whose Twitter slogan was "Just trying to keep up with the Kardashians" got her fifteen minutes all right. She pimped herself out, gamed the situation and went in for the kill. Her agent's phone was ringing off the hook.

"*Did I just ruin Tom Heaton's life via Twitter?*" she tweeted gleefully.

Most people had never even heard of Tom Heaton and no one had ever heard of Melissa, but *TMZ* never let any celebrity's obscurity or relative anonymity get in the way of a juicy story.

Angie cried and threw things at him. She went to his apartment while he was sleeping and stole all the toilet paper and tubes of adhesive he used to glue in his dental plate. Hell hath no fury. He sent flowers and called and emailed a hundred times.

"*i love you so much. there's nothing i can do about it…*" he wrote. "*everything you said is true… how can i hope? you are my life. and you will be my life as long as i'm here… the suppleness of your skin.*"

Finally, she wrote him back.

"*what about my skin….you weirdo…..starbucks anyone???*"

"*please,*" he wrote.

"*pretty please with sugar sounds a lot better…. you need to grovel more, a lot more… you should dress up and grovel… on my way…*"

He put on his best suit, an old black silk Bill Blass number that hung just right, and his black alligator boots. Angie took her time getting there but he didn't say anything when he met her at the door with Rowena already leashed.

"I dressed to grovel," he said, and she hugged him and they kissed. "You my girl?"

"I hate you," she said, holding him like she'd never let him go.

They went out through the courtyard and down the street, like they'd done most every night before all the trouble. They were happy again.

Tom hated one-dollar bills and didn't like using them. As a consequence, he had about a hundred of them in his pocket, along with fewer twenties, tens and fives. When they got to Starbucks, he handed the wad to Angie, who liked ones.

When Harris saw her come through the door he couldn't believe his luck. His first shift! She got more beautiful every time he saw her, he thought.

She ordered her Chai latte, a blueberry scone and a coffee for Tom.

"That'll be nine dollars, Angie," he said, writing her name on the paper cup he'd pour her tea in. She pulled Tom's wad from her brown leather jacket and counted out nine.

"Wow," Harris said. "That's a lot of ones."

"Yeah… It was a good night at Jumbo's," she said suggestively.

She was fucking with him, of course. She had in fact worked Jumbo's Clown Room once, but not as a stripper. Some band from Scotland shot a video there a couple of years ago and she was the girl in it.

"You work at the Clown Room? What nights are you there?"

She laughed and tipped him a buck. She was still laughing when she came out onto the patio. She told Tom about it and they both laughed.

It was a perfect LA night, the moon full and the stars bright, a warm gentle breeze and the scent of roses and jasmine in the air. They were happy. Angie set the drinks and the scone for Rowena on the table. Tom lit a cigarette and drank from his coffee.

"I love you," he said.

"I love you and I'll always love you," she said. "But you can't keep putting me through this. I can't take it."

She didn't say it in a mean way but in a kind of tired way that made him sad.

"I know," he said.

"I won't sit by and watch you kill yourself. And I won't let you humiliate me in public. I can't."

"Excuse me, sir…" It was Harris, speaking with an authority and passive aggressive manner not uncommon among nine-dollar-an-hour service workers in the hospitality industry. "There's no smoking out here on the patio."

His first shift and already the chance to show this bum up for the loser he was in front of her. Tom smiled and dropped the cigarette and crushed it under his foot.

"You know, that's so stupid," Angie said to Harris. "We're the only ones even sitting out here."

"I don't make the rules, Angie. That would be the Los Angeles County Health Department."

"And where in the fuck do you get off calling me by my first name?" she demanded.

It was as if Harris had been struck by lightning. He didn't know what to say or do. He looked at Tom.

"She doesn't even smoke, dude," Tom smiled at the guy.

"You're so perfect you should date yourself," he said to Angie in a low voice.

"I mean, it's just fucking ridiculous," Angie said, gesturing toward the line of taxicabs idling by the curb. "You've got ten cars running over there and you're worried about his goddamn cigarette?"

Harris had yet to regain his composure.

"We go to the Starbucks on Los Feliz all the time and they never say anything to us about smoking," she added.

"I'm... I'm just doing my job," Harris sputtered, walking away quickly and disappearing inside the store.

Tom lit another cigarette. "C'mon, let's get out of here," he said. They stood up and he kissed her gently.

"That was the guy," she said.

"What guy?"

"The guy who thinks I work at Jumbo's."

Tom laughed.

They walked back down Vermont, past the losers and wanna-be poseurs congregating in front of the Figaro -- an overpriced dive with delusions of Saint Germaine -- sipping espresso and munching escargot, taking themselves way too seriously.

But even they couldn't spoil the perfect beautiful night.

***

Back at Starbucks, Harris went into the restroom and smashed his forehead into the cinderblock wall. *Why do you always have to be so stupid? What do you care if the asshole was smoking? How could you be so fucking stupid?* All he could do was pray for another chance and hope to make it up to her. *Stupid. Stupid. Stupid...*

He had to remember. He wasn't dealing with Jack in the Box customers here. These were people who had accomplished things in life. Important people. Harris thought about how he'd like to get that asshole Heaton alone for five minutes so he could show him just how important he thought he was.

His hands were trembling as he took the medication out of his pocket. He only took two, and then he splashed some cold water on his face.

Why would she stick up for him like that when she knew he was running around with some 28-year-old lingerie model whore in Pasadena? Harris wondered. *She could obviously do so much better.*

But now that he'd found out that Angie danced at Jumbo's, it would be easy enough to hang around there until he ran into her. They must be doing some kind of celebrity stripper thing, he thought. He hadn't been there in awhile and the thought of seeing her like that excited him.

***

Sunday morning they drove down Sunset to Dusty's for breakfast. Tom hadn't had his coffee yet but Angie was already pretty wound up.

"And if you even think of looking at that tacky bitch walking down the street in a miniskirt at nine in the morning because she fucked some guy she met in a bar last night and can't find her car now…" she began.

"What is wrong with you?" he asked.

He was paying for crimes committed before he knew her, crimes he had not yet conceived. Everything was different when you had a woman, he thought. And everything was different in LA.

***

Rachel didn't recognize the number but she answered it anyway.

"Hello?"

"Hi, Rachel, Rachel Heaton?"

"Yes. Who's this?"

"Rachel, this is Joey Carson, and I'm a producer with the television program *Cheaters*. Are you familiar with the show?"

"Is that still on?" she asked.

"Right now we're a nationally syndicated show airing in

most markets in the United States, as well as more than a hundred countries around the world," Joey Carson said.

"I've seen it," she said. "How did you get this number?"

"Well, maybe you know why I'm calling then, Rachel. Your husband, Tom Heaton, is the writer, am I right?"

"Yes."

"You probably know then that, just last week, he was involved in kind of a mini-scandal involving a twenty-eight-year-old lingerie model out there in Pasadena and..."

"Of course I know," she said. "I'm not an idiot."

"You can't be too happy then about the fact that he's out there propositioning young models while you..."

"No actually, I'm not. I'm not happy with anything about him. Not one single thing."

"Let me ask you then, Rachel, were you thinking of pursuing any legal action against your husband?"

"It's crossed my mind," she said annoyed. "What do you want? What are we talking about here? Get to the point, would you?"

"What we were thinking... We have a detective agency we work with out there in Los Angeles, and they have young women in their employ who are pretty adept at getting cheaters like your husband to incriminate themselves..."

"A decoy, you mean?"

"Yes. That's it exactly. Now, we're going to be in New York next week and I was hoping you and I could get together and..."

"I'll talk to you. Sure I will. But you're not going to need any decoy," Rachel said. "He's been shacked up out there for the last seven months with some washed up pinup girl named Angie Roscelli."

"You're kidding," he said, writing Angie's name down on the yellow pad in front of him.

"The fucking bitch stole my husband. It's all over the

106

internet. What kind of private detectives do you have, anyway?"

Carson's head began to swim. They'd really been scraping the bottom of the barrel on *Cheaters* after twelve seasons, white trash and, hell, the truth was they were lucky when they could get white people. Before he even hung up he had already typed Angie's name into Google.

An aging Hollywood glamour girl and a D-List book writer fresh off a sexy young New York model's ugly publicity stunt? For a poverty row show like *Cheaters*, that was reality television gold. Season premiere, and a two-part episode for sure. Maybe it could get them back on *FOX* even.

Carson would call the detective agency later, punching in the number of a Hollywood casting director he knew instead. He had to find out who represented Melissa Totten and Angie Roscelli. If he could get one or both of them to do the show for money, the whole thing would go a lot easier.

He enjoyed manipulating people, experimenting on them, pushing them into public and pubic contortions for the entertainment of brain dead morons the world over. It came naturally to him.

As she hung up the phone, Rachel took a sip of her Bombay and tonic and looked out the big window. A storm had come in, one of those late afternoon soakers that pound Manhattan at rush hour, a deluge that would short out subway lines and ruin who knew how many pairs of expensive shoes. A bolt of lightning shattered the sky and the thunderclap seemed to shake the building.

CHAPTER SEVENTEEN

Tom's book – *Mexican Bloodbath* – came out in August. The few reviews it got ranged from dismissive to brutal and he started drinking again. The *New York Times* ignored it completely, but the *Los Angeles Times* summed it up in a single paragraph.

"It's unfortunate that a subject as critical as the Mexican drug war has been left to a writer as self absorbed as Heaton, who seems to think that the most significant thing about the violence that has thus far claimed nearly 50,000 lives is that some of it occurred while he was drinking at the bar of a Guadalajara whorehouse," it said.

Even his hometown paper, the *Albany Times-Union*, was ruthless. The first paid writing he'd ever done had been covering high school sports for the *Times-Union* when he was seventeen.

"Take some bad Hemingway, add a bit of Hunter Thompson at his late period worst and you've got Tom Heaton, whose Mexican Bloodbath offers a clichéd look at an important topic," the critic wrote.

"We would implore the government of Mexico to refuse Heaton further entry into their beautiful but tragic land, if only to spare the rest of us the horror, the horror of having to read any more of his writing about it," she added.

"Of course it's self absorbed," Tom yelled. "It's a goddamn memoir!"

"Fucking cunt," Angie said when he showed it to her. "I would hurt her."

She took to showing up at his place unannounced, bringing a watermelon or some avocadoes, bananas or grapes, and making coffee. If he was sleeping or in the bathroom she would take the Stolichnaya out of the freezer and dump it down the kitchen sink, refilling the bottle with water and putting it back where she'd found it.

Listening to him snore in the other room, she sat down at his computer and got on her Facebook pages, posting the Amazon link where her five thousand "friends" and ten thousand fans could buy the book. She did it repeatedly, several times every day so that it would keep going back to the top of people's news feeds.

Angie was turning down work right and left. It was getting so she couldn't pay her own bills. She stopped talking to her friends because they all just told her to get the hell away from Tom and she still hadn't gotten around to coloring her hair.

His phone rang while he was passed out that afternoon and she picked it up. It was Hank, Tom's agent back in New York. She liked Hank, and poured her heart out to him.

"I know the reviews have been rotten, Angie, but the thing is, the book's not doing that badly," Hank said. "I honestly don't know what he's so upset about."

"It's selling?"

"It's not going to make the *Times* list but yeah, it's doing all right," he said. "That business down in Pasadena helped, and the stuff you're doing on Facebook is definitely having an impact."

"Did you tell him?"

"I can't talk to him when he's like this, Angie. You don't know how thankful I was when he moved to LA."

She laughed a little. Grimly.

"I'll bet you were," she said. "I ought to be on the payroll."

"Anyway, don't say anything to him, but we got a call from Andrew Rudnick at UTA. Somebody over there's interested in optioning the book."

"UTA? With like Johnny Depp?"

"And Owen Wilson and Tim Robbins and the Coen brothers and about a thousand other biggies. It wouldn't be all that much, twenty, thirty thou maybe, but..."

"When do you think you'll know?"

"If it's going to happen, maybe six weeks. The deal would be done in ninety days."

"It would mean everything to him, Hank."

"I'll do my best, Angie," he said. "But you know as well as I do he doesn't make it easy sometimes."

***

She was washing the dishes when Tom walked in, a sink full of cups and glasses and spoons. She looked over but he didn't say anything, just walked over to the refrigerator, opened the freezer door and took out the bottle of Stoli and drank. He choked on the water.

"Goddammit, you said you were going to stop doing that," he said.

"Something wrong?" she smiled.

"OK, you win. I'm not going to do this anymore."

"What, we're breaking up?"

"No. I'm stopping now. I was getting tired of going to the liquor store anyway," he said.

He couldn't even keep the coffee down so she put him back to bed and left. When she called the next day he was up and writing and by his voice she could tell he hadn't had a drink. Still, deep down, she didn't know how much more she could take.

***

"Wow. Harris. You're standing behind a cash register wearing a green apron and a dorky black hat. How goes it, Starbucks boy?"

Tony's grin stretched from ear to ear. His crooked yellow

110

teeth glistened with saliva.

Jimmy, the twenty-something shift manager, was watching him like a hawk. There was nothing he could do. Tony had come in to bust his balls and Harris could only cast a hateful look across the bar.

It had been a bad day, starting with his first customer, some blonde chick on the phone who was apparently planning her Cabo vacation that was apparently starting in like an hour, discussing flight plans and bikinis and what time are you getting to the airport with twenty other people waiting in line behind her, and about every other sentence she would stop and apologize to the person she was talking to on the phone to shoot a nasty look toward Harris and say, "Didn't you get my order yet?"

He had no idea what she wanted. All she'd said was "venti caramel," and that could have applied to any number of menu items.

"A venti caramel *what?*" Harris pleaded. "A venti caramel *what?*"

And at the exact same second she hung up her phone, Jimmy the manager appeared at his shoulder.

"Is there a problem here Miss?" Jimmy asked.

"I asked for a venti caramel macchiato," she said. "Is he new? Because I like come in here all the time."

"Coming right up, Miss," Jimmy smiled.

"And could he not make it?" she said. "He didn't even know what it was."

"I'll make it myself, Miss."

The girl smiled at Jimmy in a way no girl had ever smiled at Harris in his whole life.

"Why don't you go hit the trash cans on the patio," Jimmy told Harris.

He could feel the headache starting then, splitting up from the back of his neck, and it only got worse after he finished the trash can detail, when Jimmy asked to see him in the office.

"Dog, when Starbucks says 'we,' it means something to us, and it means something to all the millions of people who support us. Even our name means something. You know we took it out of *Moby Dick,* right?"

"No, I…"

"Herman Melville wrote *Moby Dick,* which a lot of people say is the greatest American novel of all time," Jimmy said, pausing for a second so the significance wasn't lost.

"Tell me something man, what is it that you do?" he said then.

Harris thought for a second.

"I'm not sure what you mean, Jimmy," he said.

Jimmy looked at him soulfully.

"I mean what do you *really* do? What do you want your life to be? I'm a writer, and as soon as my shift ends I'm back in Silver Lake sitting in front of the computer. I've written four screenplays in just this last year."

"Hey, that's…" Harris began.

"Seth out there plays bass in a smokin' band, they're gonna be huge, and you know the little Asian girl, Kizu?"

Harris nodded.

"She's an amazing performance artist, very organic, very LA now. She did this thing two weeks ago on Sunset about the depictions of queer women in popular culture that was just amazing."

Harris had no idea where this was all going. There was an awkward silence.

"So?" Jimmy said finally.

"I'm not sure what…" he began.

"I mean *what is it that you do?* Because we all do something else. Because nobody who works at Starbucks just wants to work at Starbucks."

Harris was speechless. Stunned. It couldn't be. This wasn't

something he was willing to accept.

And now Tony was grinning at him across the counter as Jimmy hovered menacingly nearby. What Harris really wanted to do was strangle the two of them. His shift was nearly over and the headache was excruciating now. He tried to force a smile but could manage only a grimace.

"What can I get you?" he asked Tony.

***

When Angie was gone, Tom would wait until it got dark and cool out before clipping Rowena's pink leash onto the matching collar depicting the saints and taking her for a walk.

People mostly don't put curtains on their windows in Hollywood – not like back east where the vast expanses of heavy fabric serve as much to keep out the cold as they do for any decorative purpose – and he'd walk the neighborhood, Franklin and Commonwealth and Prospect and Kingswell, looking in people's windows not with any prurient interest but simply as a student of life, observing the natives in their natural habitat.

Whole families, huddled over various work stations scattered throughout the house, Mom and Big Sis on a MacBook Pro at the dining room table, Junior in a sort of study nook with an old and archaic looking PC, and Dad in his living room easy chair playing with his iPhone.

Doesn't anybody watch television anymore? Tom wondered. At least that was something families once did together. But on his walks with Rowena he saw that the digital Balkanization that had previously destroyed the music business and much of the print publishing industry was insidiously working its malign magic on the American family itself, eliminating shared experience that once characterized society's most elemental component.

"'Tis a sad day, Rowena old girl," he said, stopping to light a cigarette. "They're not even fucking arguing."

CHAPTER EIGHTEEN

"The doctor is IN! The doctor is IN! Medical marijuana is LEGAL in the state of California and the doctor is IN!"

A black huckster wearing a white lab coat strutted up and down the gold starred Hollywood Boulevard sidewalk in front of an open storefront, a former cocktail lounge across from the pink ghastliness of the old Hudson Apartments.

"The doctor is IN!"

Tom approached him.

"I need a card?" he asked.

"That is not a problem," the huckster said. "Because the doctor is IN!"

He led Tom into the dark lacquered lobby and handed him a clipboard and a pen then motioned him toward an old black leather sofa. Tom sat down and began filling out the questionnaire, contact information and a bare bones medical history as the huckster stepped back out onto the sidewalk and resumed his spiel, sidling up to college boys from Texas and other likely prospects.

When he got done filling out the form he handed it back to the guy, who told him that the whole deal would cost two fifty and Tom said no problem so the huckster led him back to a kind of receptionist's office where a cute Latina wearing a tight, low cut black T shirt with cutoff jeans and a pair of strappy wedge sandals sat at a makeshift desk that had been made out of what had once been a booth in a bar. She took his credit card and rang it up, then led him down a dark hall, past a dignified Alaskan malamute with the palest blue eyes he ever saw to the doctor's office.

"Jack Davis," the doctor said, holding out his hand. He was thin and kind of nervous looking. Tom introduced himself and shook hands with him. They sat down at a cheap desk and the doctor took his blood pressure. The machine wasn't working right and the doctor had to redo it several times.

"What's the condition you're hoping to treat with cannabis?" Jack asked.

"Stress, anxiety and insomnia," Tom said, looking at the diplomas and license on the wall and seeing that Jack actually was an MD and not some kind of crazy osteopath or chiropractor. What was his fucking story? Eight years at UCLA and an emergency room internship at Hollywood Presbyterian for this? Seriously. For a guy like him, this was one step up from biting the heads off chickens in a freak show.

The doctor then told him not to smoke medical marijuana in the car because that was a crime or even have it in the glove box because that was a crime too. He told him not to take it onto any federal property, including airports, FBI offices or national parks and pretty much just be careful out there.

He signed a document and folded it and put it into a regular business envelope.

"There you go," he said.

The document gave Tom the inalienable right to legally have up to a half-pound of dope stashed around his house at any given time, to buy an ounce every day and to smoke himself stupid anytime the mood struck him.

Maybe it would help.

***

"On tonight's episode of Homeless or Famous? ... She drives a Cadillac... But it barely runs! Her clothes look expensive, but she's been wearing them for fifteen years!

"Is she...?"

"HOMELESS," the studio audience chimed in.

"OR...

"FAMOUS?!?!?!?!"

Harris sat sweating on the couch in his boxer shorts and T-shirt nursing a glass of Black Velvet and eating a burrito from 7-11. He'd seen the episode before. It was Erin Moran, the little sister from the old "Happy Days" show.

But even if he hadn't already seen it, it would have been hard to concentrate on the show. He was confused. Jimmy's words tore at him.

"Nobody who works at Starbucks just wants to work at Starbucks."

Maybe Jimmy was just a bad seed. Maybe he'd seen so much in his own climb up the corporate ladder that he'd become jaded and cynical, forgetting all he had been a part of, *Our Starbucks* – one person, one cup, one neighborhood at a time. It wasn't just a job, it was passion, full of friendship and respect and dignity. It was all about uplifting people's lives and establishing human connections. In the end, it wasn't about the coffee, it was about humanity. That's why Our Starbucks mattered, it was full of humanity.

Sure, that was it, Harris thought, he'd seen it at Jack in the Box. A rising young star shoots up from the counter to become a team leader then the assistant manager inside of a year, and all of a sudden it's like that song, "Is that all there is?" They get bored, they get testy, they start looking for a way out. That was it. He just happened to arrive as Jimmy began melting down. Clearly, the pressure had gotten to the kid.

That must have been it, Harris thought coldly. Because if that wasn't it, there was only one other possibility. And that was that he himself was a fool, that the world had played him for a fool again and that he walked right into it, like he always did, stupidly, with his eyes wide open.

He had gone for so long believing there was no good, there was no evil. There was only what was, and that it meant nothing. He believed that we were without purpose, that anyone who thought they were living a purposeful life was lying to himself. Because there were no plans, no decisions, no choices. No free will, ultimately. There was just dumb fucking luck.

But that all changed when he found Starbucks. When he found Angie. After what seemed like a lifetime of searching, Harris found his good and evil, and he again found the sense of purpose he lost one afternoon on a dusty street in Baghdad back in April, 2003.

"How do you tell a man and his wife you're sorry you killed their son?" Harris had screamed at the VA doctors. *"What do you SAY?!?!?!"*

And no matter what he did he couldn't get those broken faces out of his head. The kid's dead eyes and the blood all over. His mistake. His fuckup. Sometimes he dreamed about it and would wake up thinking for a second that it had only been a nightmare, and that he was all right. But he wasn't all right and it wasn't a nightmare. It all happened and there was nothing he could do to take it back. His hands were shaking and his head hurt so bad. He reached for his medication on the coffee table.

"Life hasn't been kind to Erin Moran since the foreclosure of her California home," the television announcer said. *"To look at Erin today you'd never know she was once one of TV's biggest stars. Her peaches-and-cream complexion has turned into a maze of wrinkles and crow's feet. She's aged terribly."*

The funny thing, ironic thing, was that Erin Moran, it turned out, was both famous *and* close to homeless at the time the episode was shot, so it was almost like a trick question. She and her day laborer husband were living in a ramshackle trailer park somewhere in the Midwest, it was revealed, and there'd been a breast flashing incident at a local tavern.

"Erin was drinking and was having fun with some friends when someone dared her to flash her boobs," the barmaid they interviewed said. *"She didn't want to do it, but her husband and*

them kept after her and she like quickly lifted her T-shirt."

"But other than her few friends, no one recognized her," the announcer said sadly. "Most of the customers were scratching their heads and asking, 'What was that all about?' and 'Who the heck is Erin Moran?'"

The bigger they are, the harder they fall, Harris thought. Jimmy's bad attitude would be noticed, if it hadn't been already, and his removal would give Harris the opportunity he was looking for. In a year he'd be running the place.

He went into the bedroom and put on the suit he bought for the interview. It was nearly 10 o'clock, time for the shift change at Jumbo's Clown Room. He'd been there every night for a week and still hadn't managed to catch Angie.

He longed to see her there, that hot little body, creamy thighs and ass, her soft white skin, the expression on her face and those eyes, those liquid green eyes. The way her raven hair fell around her shoulders and her nails painted midnight blue. It overwhelmed him just to think about it. He supposed how it would be, sitting there when she came out, and he thought about her dexterity on the pole. But mostly he thought about stuffing a ten-dollar bill into her thong.

That would be heaven. Heaven on earth.

***

It had all been Angie's idea, of course, the medical marijuana, the twice weekly AA meetings at the church on the corner of Fairfax and Fountain, a holistic approach to an age old problem, like a television announcer might say. And Tom didn't say a thing about her using the meetings – which she insisted on attending with him – to chat up every casting director, agent and half baked promoter in the room, networking shamelessly, using, turning other people's addictions to her own advantage. Nor did he mention the fact that she smoked as much of the doctor dope as he did.

Instead he kept his mouth shut, did what she wanted him to do and left her alone when they went to bed at night. She seemed almost contented, but it didn't stop her from issuing threats on an almost hourly basis, what would happen if he took a drink, what would happen if he spoke to Rachel, what would happen if he did this or that or the other thing. Still, as long as she got exactly what she wanted all the time, Angie could seem reasonably happy.

Which was what made Tom happy at that point.

She'd been there for a few days, smoking pot, eating fruit and talking, falling deeper and deeper in love. He held her when she wanted to be held and kissed her whatever way she wanted him to and, after she'd fallen asleep beside him on the couch, her head resting on his belly like it was a pillow, he'd say, "Hey Slim, let's go to bed," and walk her into the bedroom and put her under the covers.

That morning they got up early. She was working later.

"Read me the horoscopes," she said, sipping her tea. "I want to see what's going on."

She was lying across the black couch and he sat at his work desk in an old lacquered chair. He clicked to the horoscopes.

"Yours first," she said.

He clicked onto the extended daily forecast for Aquarius and read aloud. About two sentences in, he realized he shouldn't have.

"*Are you bored with someone and not sure how to break it to them? Then don't,*" the horoscope read. "*They don't necessarily need to know that they are becoming tedious to you – it will only hurt their feelings and make you look uncaring, which is not who you are. Instead, just get some time away from them. You don't have to explain why you are suddenly busy every time they ask you to hang out. After enough time has passed, you can start socializing with them again. You just need a break, and that is okay.*"

"That doesn't even make any sense," Angie said. "You don't even hang out with anybody..."

"I don't know," he said.

A black light went on over Angie's head. It illuminated things not visible to the naked eye.

"Wait a minute... Becoming *tedious* to you?" she said.

"I didn't say it. That's what it said."

"You need a *break?*"

"Would you stop it?" Tom laughed. "Just stop it."

"I don't want you to ever read that horoscope again. Fuck those people and their horoscope. You can find a different horoscope to read!"

He got another cup of coffee and went outside for a cigarette. He walked back in the kitchen and shut the door behind him. She called from the bathroom. "Baby..."

She was sitting on the toilet, pissing, her sheer black slip hiked up around her hips and she said, "Get over here."

He did as he was told and she looked up into his eyes then reached over and undid the Gucci belt she'd gotten him, unbuttoned the Levis 501s she favored and pulled out his cock, which was still swollen and heavy from sleeping next to her and not jumping on her for several nights running. She leaned forward and put it in her mouth, moving up and down on it, licking and sucking, and he put out his hand and leaned on the sink to keep from falling down. "Jesus Christ," he said, and she made a pleasant sound. When he came his knees all but went out from under him and she was pissing and he reached down and cupped his hand between her legs, allowing her piss to fill it, and she swallowed his cum and looked up at him, and he pulled his hand away up from her pussy. Her piss dripped off it and onto the black and white tiled floor. He put as much of it as he could into his mouth and it tasted so sweet. She still held his cock in her hand, petting it, and he held her by the shoulders and leaned over and kissed her on the top of the head.

She got up off the couch and dug in her purse for the keys.

"I've got to go to work," she said. "Try and stay out of trouble."

"Oh. I will," he said. "I will."

He kissed her at the door, a peck on the cheek, and she was off, like some career girl in a romantic comedy from the 1940s.

CHAPTER NINETEEN

Another idea Angie had was that Tom should go see his mother, who lived with his father and his brother on top of a mountain west of Louisville, Kentucky. His mother hadn't been well, and Angie thought that maybe Tom could gain some insight or maybe even resolve some issues by talking them out with his family.

She didn't know about his family, of course, the suicides, the murder, the alcoholism and drug addiction, the various and undiagnosed mental problems and unspecific anti-social behavior. She'd never experienced the deafening silence in which these things and more were not talked about by the actors themselves when they all sat together in a room.

She hadn't a clue how the family became so desperately poor or why they refused to take anything from Tom. She didn't know, couldn't know, but that wasn't her fault, and Angie had decided he should go see his mother.

And so – against his better judgment – that morning he found himself waiting for the airport taxi in front of the house. Angie looked gorgeous in a short and clingy lavender chiffon dress, the gauzy material hugging every curve and her nipples plainly visible underneath.

The cab pulled up and they stood necking on the sidewalk. Then Angie picked Rowena up to lick his face goodbye.

"Beautiful," said the cab driver, a Russian, eyeing Angie as Tom got in and shut the door.

"Yeah. I don't know if I like the woman better or the dog," Tom said, lighting a cigarette.

"You lucky man," the driver said.

"Yes."

He'd always been lucky. He took a cigarette out of the pack

as the driver headed down Vermont toward the 101. He hoped his luck would hold.

***

The call came about fifteen minutes after Tom arrived.

His father, with whom he had never gotten along, lie on the bed staring at the ceiling. His brother, Tom's uncle and the only person in the family the old man would still talk to, was dead of cancer. He'd had it for a while, it went into remission, it came back.

"David hated Dad," Tom's father said of his brother.

"And it was all over one beating."

Tom said nothing, and the old man began to cry quietly.

"I never told you about it... David and I had been down swimming at White City Beach – I don't remember how we even got down there, but we went in swimming and there were turds and used rubbers and toilet paper and everything else floating in that water because that's where the sewage emptied out into Lake Erie.

"And we got home and Dad found out. He was so mad... He started beating on me, I was scared to death of him and started bawling the first time he hit me almost, but then he started beating David. And David wouldn't cry and Dad got madder and madder and beat him worse and worse...

"I was screaming..."

The old man's face twisted grotesque with pain at the thought of it and the tears streamed down his face. It had been sixty years since that beating but now, for the old man, it was as though it just happened.

Tom was quiet, watching him, wanting to hug him but knowing the old man would consider it inappropriate.

124

"After that, David didn't have much use for the old man, or ma either," his father said. "And it was all over that one beating."

"David was tough as nails," Tom said after awhile.

There was no talk of going back home for the funeral; none of them believed in God and David had willed his body to scientific research. The old man didn't call anyone and wouldn't talk to his other brother or his sisters when they called the house. Everybody was left alone to deal with the family tragedy.

That was the kind of family they had. They were all tough as nails. Crazy stupid tough. Tom looked at the old man crying on the bed, the father with whom he had never gotten along, and remembered the beatings he and his own brother took from him.

"C'mon out, let's have a cup of coffee," Tom said.

"I'll be out in a minute," the old man said, wiping his eyes.

When he came out of the bedroom, the old man was composed, almost like nothing had happened.

"You all right?" Tom asked.

"I'd be better if it was you that was dead," his father said, getting a cup from out of the dishwasher.

***

Tom's brother was a brain damaged alcoholic and former drug addict who had sponged off their elderly mother and father from the day he was born. He was now fifty, balding and already smelling like an old man, a hundred pounds overweight and gay, even though he hadn't had a boyfriend in more than twenty years. He earned a little more than minimum wage as a short order cook at the neighborhood Shoney's and lived in an ancient, rotting cottage languishing in an obscure corner of the parents' modest acreage.

125

Charles hated Tom as much as their father did. He hated Tom and most other successful people too, since Charles, like their father, was the sort of hopeless failure who has to believe the entire system is corrupt, fixed and set up to keep astonishing individuals such as themselves from reaching their true potential.

Tom hugged Charles when he saw him the next morning and suggested that he take him and their mother out to lunch. The old man had feigned a back injury early that morning to get out of going anywhere. Charles said he had to get ready first so Tom and his mother waited and waited and finally his brother emerged from his decrepit and rotting cottage weeping because he was so ugly and fat and had a stupid job and no friends or money to buy clothes with, and Tom and their mother had nice clothes. He wasn't going, he said.

"You two go have a good time," he sniffed.

"I'll be OK." He broke down sobbing.

Actually, he went out in public all the time despite the fact he looked like a carnival circuit wrestler, but now that Tom had come to see his mother, his brother couldn't deal with it not being all about him.

So the old man was crying and Charles was crying and Ma, who was the one Tom had been concerned about in the first place and whose health he had come in particular to check on, was, in the end, the only sane and healthy person there. They succeeded in making his mother feel bad though, and since she felt so sorry for them she didn't much feel like doing anything either.

Tom was stuck there. For three days he listened to his father tell him that all writing, and especially his writing, was bullshit and that only an asshole would want to live in Los Angeles. It was hotter than hell in Los Angeles, he said, citing a couple of days he spent there in the summer of 1952, when he was in the Navy. He asked whether Angie was an American citizen because it seemed to him that the only reason a girl like her would go with a loser like Tom would be to get a green card.

In all the time he was there, Tom never once wondered why he left home when he was sixteen or why he hadn't been back in the last five years. He spoke to his mother every week on the telephone, at least, but the rest of it was really just fucking depressing.

***

On the second afternoon, he took his mother into town to do some grocery shopping. On the way back, they stopped at a diner for pie and coffee.

"When I look back on my life, my married life, it's in two parts," she said. "The first twenty-five years were like a dream. Dad was making good money, I was making good money, we had you kids and the house in Albany… We had a great life.

"But then Dad lost his job and everything went bad after that. We sold the house and moved out here… It was a terrible decision, but what can you do? You can't go get the house back after somebody else bought it. I cried my eyes out every night for a year. I hated it here so bad."

"I know, Ma," he said.

"You just have to live with it, and that's what I've been doing for the last twenty-five years, the second half," she said.

"Living with it."

His mother had been glamorous and remained striking in a Joan Didion sort of way, though her hair had turned white and she'd given up on coloring it some time ago. She'd made her own choices, falling in love as a young girl with a guy who looked promising but couldn't go the distance. And then staying with him, even after it had all fallen apart.

"I'll tell you one thing," she said from behind the Jackie O.

sunglasses she still wore. "If he goes first, I'll be out of here so fast it'll make your head spin."

Tom smiled broadly but she was deadly serious. She turned her head and looked away from him for a moment. Then the waitress came and brought the coffee and strawberry pie they'd ordered. When his mother turned back to him, she was smiling too.

"That looks so good!" she said.

***

"What do you do?" the father asked on the third morning as Tom walked from one room into another. The father had been essentially unemployed for the past twenty-seven years, and dragged as many family members as humanly possible down into the gutter of poverty with him. He dragged Tom's mother down into it and Tom would never forgive him for that.

"What do I do?"

"You heard me. What do you do?"

"I try to be a good person and stay happy," he managed with a straight face. His father turned a beet red and sat forward in his chair.

"A job, Tom. Do you work? I mean do you work?"

"I always work, Dad," Tom said. "The Mexican book just came out, I've got a novel going."

He knew that his father did not consider the writing of books to be work, no matter how hard they were to write or how much money was made off them. To him, authors were shiftless, lazy, egotistical bums, making up stories and offering their worthless opinions up for the amusement of other, similarly dispositioned individuals called readers.

It was all just triviality.

"Because if you didn't work you'd be like me," the father said.

"No Dad, I don't think I would," Tom said. "Be like you, I mean."

CHAPTER TWENTY

He longed for the reality of Hollywood.

On the plane back to LA the minutes passed like hours as he tried to get the bad taste of the trip out of his mouth and off his soul and out of his head. There was only Angie, waiting for him at his apartment, beautiful and beatific. He'd never leave her again, he swore to himself. It was never any good when he did.

She emailed him just before he boarded:

"be good... i'm sending all my angels to keep u safe... soon my love... soon... no one and nothing else matters when it comes to us and our love....it's not only dangerous and intoxicating.....but it flies and is protected by the goddesses of love and light.....shut up shut up all those crazies, voices in your head....they can't touch you as long as u stay in the light....so keep those fake shades on..."

But when he got home she wasn't there. He called the number a couple of times and got the answering machine. So he went in and lay down on the bed with the dog Rowena and tried in vain to sleep. At last, with daylight streaming through the cracks between the shades, he drifted off only to be immediately roused by the sound of the front door opening.

"C'mon and buy me breakfast," she said. "I'm starving."

Rowena didn't budge. Tom did, only slightly.

"Where were you?" he asked.

"What do you mean where was I? I was home," she said.

"I thought you were coming over last night."

"I started playing with the puppy," she said. "And then my sister called and I had to talk to her."

"I called a couple of times."

"I fell asleep on the couch. I was watching a movie. Are we getting breakfast or not?"

He got out of bed and walked past her into the bathroom.

"Are you mad? Are you gonna be mad? Because I don't even want to go if you're gonna be mad," she said.

Tom stared in the bathroom mirror sucking down a Lucky Strike. His father had wished him dead, and now this.

"If we're going we have to go now because I have to meet a client at 10:30," she said a moment later.

***

Harris sat on a hard chair in his bedroom, looking down at the disassembled weapon on the bed. Basically a scaled down Kalashnikov rifle action designed to fire pistol ammunition, the PPSh-41 was a semi-automatic version of a popular Soviet submachine gun manufactured in Poland to help fill the need for an economically affordable assault weapon in the voracious American market.

With an old toothbrush and some Hoppe's No. 9 Solvent, he removed every speck of grease and old oil from each of the parts before wiping them down with a handkerchief sprayed lightly with Miltech-1, a dry impregnating lubricant favored among the troops in Iraq and Afghanistan.

He'd of course become familiarized with the Kalashnikov system while on active duty over there. The AK-47 was the chief battle rifle of the bad guys, and – like a lot of American soldiers – he'd come to respect it more than the M4 standard issue carbine. After he was discharged, he saw the PPSh-41 in the window of a gun shop over on Central Avenue and ended up taking it and two hundred and fifty rounds of the exotic 7.65x25mm ammunition it fired home with him for just over three hundred dollars.

As he finished oiling the pieces, he clicked them back into place, reassembling the weapon. He pulled the trigger, throwing the heavy bolt down past the lips of the empty magazine to the mouth of the chamber. He set it back in its hard shell case, along with the four 32-round magazines he'd loaded previously.

***

Rachel woke up and got a beer out of the refrigerator. She was already crying, so she slumped down on the kitchen tile and let herself go, wailing, watching herself from the inside.

I've got to pull myself together. I've got to do better, she told herself, as she had every day since childhood, except when she managed to drown the hypercritical demon in her mind with booze. She took the grocery lister off the refrigerator door and began.

1.) Be prettier and thinner than his girlfriend, or at least as much.

a/ Lean Cuisine
b/ Tooth veneers
c/ Colored contact lenses
d/ Dermabrasion

2.) Have a better job.

a/ Conde Nast
b/ Knopf

3.) Have a better boyfriend.
a/ Hugh Laurie
b/ Leonard Cohen
c/ Anthony Bourdain
d/ Russell Brand

4.) Live in a better city

a/ ~~New York~~
b/ ~~Los Angeles~~
c/ London

How am I going to do all that, when I just stumbled into this? She wanted a fresh start, but she already had two master's degrees. Gone were the days when she could scam up an academic fellowship like some people sign onto welfare.

She grabbed the countertop to pull herself up and dumped a bag of Purina Cat Chow onto the floor. Then she began scooping out the litter box. The task had been neglected for some time. It's like I'm a fucking chambermaid for cats, she thought.

She took an Ativan, considered the Ambien, and then swallowed two. They wouldn't make her sleep, not this early. She opened another beer.

Her iPhone lay smashed on the kitchen floor. She dimly remembered that Angie had called last night to offer beauty tips. It was funny, because she only knew Angie from some stupid mixed-up connection the previous day. Angie had been leaving dozens of messages for Tommy on her iPhone, having somehow confused the numbers.

"Hey, that psycho bitch wife of yours keeps emailing. You need to take care of this."

Rachel had finally called to set her straight, drunkenly dumping twenty years' worth of incriminating information about her worthless husband. It wasn't really Rachel's fault. She didn't know what lies Tommy had told Angie, and Angie didn't know what lies Tommy had told Rachel, so neither of them knew what should be redacted. This became the topic of their conversation.

No one Tommy and Rachel knew had called her since the

breakup eight months ago. Not one. Now she was not only invisible to any man she encountered – their eyes slid right off her like she was a ghost – she was invisible to everyone they had known.

She thought Tommy's friends had liked her, saw her as cool, cute-looking and fun. Tommy always hung out with rock and rollers and band guys always dug her and could sniff her out in the least likely situations. The guy who made her sandwich would turn out to be a drummer in some band. She assumed they liked her because she was conversant in their world. Some kind of musician radar. She looked up some of those guys on Facebook years later and they'd all married women who looked like her.

Tommy had been in a band once too. She remembered him fretting over what he'd call his legacy. Did she think he'd be known more for his writing or his music, he had asked. She knew he wanted to hear the writing. For such a hard and often cruel person, Tommy could be surprisingly fragile and needy. She called him a raconteur one day, and that made him happy, like he'd finally gotten the book contract, won the lottery, scored the drug and nailed the girl.

Angie's follow-up call was to the point.

"Don't cut your hair. Guys like long hair. And don't wear heavy foundation. It shows your wrinkles. You look like 'Whatever Happened to Baby Jane' with all that... Hold on. I'm getting another call. Hold on a second."

The bitch never came back on the line. Rachel picked up the pieces of her iPhone and dropped them into the litter box. She opened another beer.

***

Angie lay in the shade on the grass, her face resting on her folded hands with Joel sitting on the ground next to her, rubbing her back. What was she going to do? The way she felt about Tom scared her. She hadn't given herself so completely to anyone since she was a child, sitting on the lawn in front of Hollywood High, so wild and beautiful and young. Now it scared her. She pulled back and pushed him away. He didn't understand and got angry. All he wanted was to be with her. And all she wanted was what she wanted. Joel waited in the wings with a dozen others, waiting for Tom to stumble, waiting for Angie to tire of that rough ass Hell's Kitchen bullshit and come back into the warm light of California, each of them waiting for their own chance at bliss.

"He's an asshole, Angie. He doesn't deserve someone like you."

"It's not like you're all that and a bag of chips, Joel."

She rolled her shoulder blade as he pressed his fingers in.

"Look, I'm talking to you as a friend. The guy's bad news."

"Maybe that's why I love him," she said.

"You're smarter than that, Angie," he said.

"Am I? Really?"

There was obviously a lesson to be had here, but she wasn't sure what it was.

The golden afternoon sunlight poked in patches through the leaves of the great Fremont cottonwood tree above them and the grass was lush and green and soft. She watched a young girl walking her dog up the trail and suddenly she was missing her sick little Maltese puppy and Rowena and, by extension, Tom. She caught a whiff of marijuana and shook her head softly when Joel tried to hand her the little pipe.

"I've really got to get going," she said, pushing herself up off the ground.

***

After she left, Tom tried to go back to sleep but couldn't.

He'd brought Kentucky home with him, his father and his brother, their ignorance and viciousness and spite, and he found himself counting in his head all the ways he had succeeded where they had failed. It was a stupid, dysfunctional thing to do, he knew, but he couldn't help it and smoked bowl after bowl of the medical marijuana trying to get it out of his head. After awhile he started wanting a drink and thought of walking Rowena down to Hollywood Liquors and picking up a half pint. That would be another stupid thing. Still, he had all but made up his mind when Angie walked through the front door and rushed across the room to him.

"Oh Tom, I love you so much," she said. "I want you to marry me, I do."

With Angie in his arms there was no more thought of his father or his brother or even his mother. No thought of the liquor store. No thought of the world existing or time outside the two of them at that moment. She was a miracle, his savior and he held her tight.

"I love you baby," he said. "You make me so happy."

***

In his room at the Milford Plaza in New York, "Cheaters" producer Joey Carson was ecstatic. He'd met with and signed both Tom Heaton's wronged wife Rachel and Melissa Totten, the young lingerie model Tom had tried to pick up at the bar of the Langham Hotel in Pasadena. Rachel was getting up there but Melissa was one hot monkey. Carson had decided not to approach Heaton's girlfriend Angie Roscelli at all. It would have been great to get her and she was Actor's Equity, but Carson figured it wasn't worth the risk of her tipping Heaton off ahead of time.

They would gather in Hollywood to rock Tom Heaton's world and maybe, just maybe, get a few more people to tune in to the show.

Carson hadn't decided where the ambush would take place exactly, but he had six days and would have a better handle on Heaton's routine by then.

There was an email report from the private investigator who'd been tailing Tom and Angie for the past ten days. He was bored, he said.

"These people don't do anything," the detective wrote. *"Walk the dog and get coffee early in the morning, come home. Go out to lunch at noon. Run to the post office, grocery store, dry cleaners, his bank, her bank etc. in one of four late model vehicles, go home. Walk the dog and get coffee again at night. They're asleep by 11 o'clock. This is every day. In a week I haven't seen them do anything besides eat and run errands. They're very affectionate toward each other when they do these things and I've got a lot of good candid pics, but still. These people don't do anything."*

"Must be nice," Carson said. He was looking at a picture of Angie.

***

The morning brought no relief. They were who they were no matter if they were happy or sad. All vanity and dissolution. Between them, Tom and Angie had spent nearly a century striving just to get there. And it was what it was. Another beautiful day in Tinseltown.

"Hold Everything!" her horoscope read. *"To have two events – Jupiter 90 degrees to Neptune, and Saturn virtually motionless – almost simultaneously is very unusual. Add in the Moon being parallel to Uranus as well as Mars and it is clear that surprises, shock waves and highly unpredictable events are in the hopper. Confusion and chaos are likely emanations coming from the Jupiter-Neptune face-off while Saturn motionless in its negative aspect places an emphasis on self-doubt, chronic disabilities, fear, pessimism and possibly*

depression. Take a mental health day, stay in bed and pull the covers up over your head."

God fucking America, Angie thought. What if pulling the covers up over your head was just not an option? The stars had started causing trouble back in March and now it was Augus, more than half the time they'd even been together. There'd been confusion and chaos all right, and there'd been moments of tenderness she'd only dreamt about for years.

It was just before six and already bright outside. At 10 she would drive out to Santa Monica to shoot a print ad for some jewelry company. Tom had taken a writing assignment from Dire McCain for *Paraphilia* magazine and would be working on that at home. She wouldn't see him again until dinner, and wished they were rich so they wouldn't have to work and could just stay home together.

She sat up in the bed with her laptop in front of her, wearing a black silk slip and vintage reading glasses, drinking a cranberry and lime. She was reading an article about the Biblical scholar Karen L. King – Hollis Professor of Divinity at Harvard -- who had recently discovered an ancient Coptic text that seemed to support the belief that Jesus and Mary Magdalene were husband and wife, just as the Masons had maintained for centuries. King's analysis certainty seemed convincing. Tom lay next to her asleep.

CHAPTER TWENTY-ONE

"Fuck!" Tom spat, a look of disgust crossing his face.

He recognized the guy as soon as they flashed a photo over live video of some crime scene up in the hills somewhere.

"Hollywood screenwriter Elko Houghton was found dead at his Topanga Canyon retreat early this morning following a panicked 911 call from his live-in girlfriend, Suleiman," The announcer said. *"Police were called to a Topanga Canyon residence for what had been first reported by neighbors as a domestic disturbance, we're told. When officers arrived, they found Houghton at the scene, dead of an apparent self inflicted gunshot wound to the head."*

"Fuck," he said again.

He'd talked to Hank about somebody at UTA wanting to option *Mexican Bloodbath* and Tom said he wanted to do the screenplay himself so Hank looked into it. It turned out that whoever it was at UTA who wanted the option already had some key people on board, and one of those people had been Elko Houghton. Tom was at his computer now and *TMZ* had video of the sheet-covered gurney being brought out into the daylight from underneath a carport attached to what looked like an upscale mobile home. As the shot widened and a neighbor's house appeared, Tom laughed.

"Who knew they had a trailer park in Topanga Canyon?" he asked in wonder to no one in particular.

His mind began to race. Would whomever it was at UTA still want to option the book? And, now that Houghton was dead, would Tom be able to snag the screenwriting gig? He could use the money.

As usual, Angie was five steps ahead of him. She'd been standing in the kitchen and heard the whole thing. Now, sitting on the edge of the bathtub with the exhaust fan blowing to obscure the conversation, she was talking with Hank.

"It's his story, Hank," she said. "He lived it. Who better to write the fucking movie?"

Back in the living room, Tom scratched Rowena on the head. Houghton's claim to fame was that he wrote the original screenplay for Tom Cruise's Scientology epic *Battleground Uranus*, and then been fired. Somebody else came in and redid the play, and somebody else redid it again. The film went on to be one of the biggest box office disasters in Hollywood history and Houghton came out richer and smelling like a rose.

When Angie emerged from the bathroom, Tom told her about Houghton and she acted as though she hadn't a clue.

"Maybe I'll get the screenplay now," he said.

"That would be just like what happened in *Rosemary's Baby*."

"Right? Donald Baumgartner. Tony Curtis did the voice."

"What?"

"The actor who goes blind in *Rosemary's Baby* so that John Cassavetes can get the part."

"Tony Curtis?" Angie said.

"Yeah, look it up. The guy on the phone. A lot of people just assume it was Robert Loggia."

***

He leaned in the doorway of an antiques shop on La Brea wearing his black Armani suit and woven leather Ferragamo loafers without socks smoking a joint of medical marijuana when a younger German woman approached him. She looked pleasant and carefree, wearing a yellow summer dress and wedge sandals.

"Excuse me, sir, do you have a light?" she asked.

Tom pulled the Zippo from his pants pocket and lit the cigarette the girl was holding. He didn't like the 'sir' bit.

"Thank you," she smiled.

He smiled back.

Inside the gallery, Angie chatted with Rodney Bingenheimer about a new book on the Hollywood glam scene they'd helped create some thirty-five years earlier. Each had been written about in reverential tones and the gawkers stood back ten feet or so to revel in the cool. She wore a long sleeve white lace mini-dress and strapped rhinestone platforms. She was waiting, like everybody else, for Booker T – *sans* MGs -- to take to the small stage. The space was filled with artists and writers and musicians there for the book launch, and Angie was very much in demand. She had her picture taken with Rodney and then with the rock writer Harvey Kubernick and then with Frank Infante, who played bass with Blondie after they kicked Gary Valentine out, and then with Michael Des Barres, who was the groupie memoirist Pamela Des Barres' ex-husband.

Angie was blinking from the flashes when Tom came up to her from behind and slid his arm around her waist.

"Hi baby," she said, and she kissed him.

"You're the most beautiful woman in the room," he told her.

"You know, you're not the first person who's said that to me tonight."

"I'll bet."

"No, really."

"Shut up," he said.

She pretended to straighten his shirttail but grabbed his cock instead and somebody snapped a picture. Booker T. Jones, sharp dressed and sixty-eight, made his way up from the back of the crowded room behind a security guy, sat down at the organ and slid into "Green Onions."

When he finished his set, Angie had her picture taken with him too.

Later they walked in the moonlight down Avocado Street toward Hillhurst, old Rowena setting the pace and Tom and Angie holding hands and keeping up. The night air was perfect and fragrant and when they stopped and waited to cross at Commonwealth they kissed under the streetlight there.

From behind a giant hedge on the corner came the immediately recognizable strains of a tune, being played with a charming naiveté by someone on a piano. The timeworn melody was both simple and sophisticated, something Woody Allen might use in a movie, but hearing it there in the dreamy California night was so out of context it took him a moment to think of what it was.

"I love this song," she said.

And then he remembered. Piaf. *"La Vie en rose."*

"Look Tommy, look," Angie said. She'd parted the bushes with her hands and through the opening they saw a little girl with long blonde hair, maybe ten years old, seated at an upright in front of the window. She was precious and pretty and confident.

Quand il me prend dans ses bras
Il me parle tout bas
Je vois la vie en rose

They stopped looking at the girl and he put his arms around her and they danced a few slow steps. She looked up at him and he kissed her again.

"I love you Tommy," Angie said. "Sometimes I don't want to but I can't help it."

She was fun and playful and sad all at once, and he wished he'd known her ten years earlier. Twenty. She made him happy, which was a thing he'd stopped believing was even possible a long time ago.

"I know baby, I know."

On the other side of the intersection there was a young guy walking a black cocker spaniel. Angie stopped to say how cute the dog was and tell him about Rowena. She asked the guy what veterinarian he went to and talked about the one she went to, beginning a conversation with a complete stranger that would last nine minutes and thirty-eight seconds, leaving the stranger to wonder what the hell just happened.

When Angie was a little girl she got her first dog, a beautiful cocker spaniel she named Gypsy, she said. Awhile later, her mother told her they had to move. School had just started and Angie was worried she wouldn't be able to go to the same school, but her mother said they weren't moving that far and it would be the same school. But there was one thing and that was the new apartments had a strict no dogs allowed policy.

So they moved and left Gypsy with a neighbor and once in awhile her mother would take Angie over for a visit. It was after one of these visits that the dog bolted out the neighbor's door, ran two blocks down and was run over by a car while crossing Normandie Avenue. "She went looking for Angie," the neighbor woman had cried.

Angie told the stranger all this and how she had hated her mother for the longest time because she blamed her for Gypsy's death. But time had passed and forgiving others is a big step toward healing yourself, she said.

Tom had started slowly walking away, lest the guy end up coming home and living with them. When Angie caught up with him she told him never to do that again when she was talking to someone and he said OK but he didn't really mean it.

She remembered what she'd been talking about before, and started anew.

"Anyway, I try to treat everyone like they're the most

important person in the world to me," Angie said. "Even though they're not."

Tom laughed out loud.

"Your fake sincerity is incredible," he said, smiling. "It's one of the things I love about you best."

"*It's true!*" she said and he laughed again.

***

At Starbucks they took a table on the patio near a couple of guys who turned out to be writers. They were talking about Elko Houghton. Tom handed Angie some bills and she went inside for their drinks.

"They took the girlfriend into custody?" one of the writers said.

"And get this, she's a thirty-two-year-old Ukrainian. Super hot. She's got a young son apparently, and wanted to get out of the city. They say that school district out there's one of the best in the state."

"So she gets Elko to buy her a place up in Topanga Canyon… "

"The place was on Mulholland. It wasn't really Topanga."

"Well, it's on the valley side of Topanga but it's still Topanga, I think."

"Whatever. It's Calabasas, the Beverly Hills of the Valley… Anyway, six months later he's dead, right?"

"And now she comes up with a cocktail napkin from Musso & Frank where he changes his will and leaves everything to her instead of the wife…"

Inside, Harris's heart skipped a beat when he saw Angie come through the door, ravishing in white lace with a black leather motorcycle jacket slung across her shoulders, high heels clicking on the tile.

"Hello there… Harris," she said.

"Venti Chai latte soy and grande coffee, right Angie?"

"You have a good memory."

"It's all part of the Starbucks experience," Harris said. He poured the coffee and got the tea started. "That'll be nine dollars."

Angie pulled out Tom's roll and peeled off nine ones.

"Another great night at the Clown Room?" he asked.

"Yeah," she smiled. "Something like that."

"You know, I've been going there for awhile, but I haven't seen you, Angie. When do you come on?"

"Pardon me?"

"What nights do you work, you know?"

"You don't really think I'm a stripper at Jumbo's Clown Room, do you?" Angie snapped. "Do I look like a goddamned stripper to you? And where the fuck do you get off calling me by my first name? I told you not to do that."

"Well, you said…"

"Jesus Christ."

"And even if I was a stripper I sure as hell wouldn't be dancing at the Clown Room. It's insulting."

She took the coffee and went out to Tom.

"That guy in there? He thinks I really am a stripper!" she said to him.

"You told him you were."

"Do I look like a stripper to you?"

"Somebody's idea of a stripper, maybe."

"What the hell's that supposed to mean?"

"Just that maybe, I don't know, in somebody's fantasy or whatever…"

"Do I look like a stripper? Do you think I look like a stripper? *I want to know!*"

"No. I think you're the most beautiful girl in Hollywood. The most beautiful girl who ever lived."

"You say that."

"It's true."

She knew it was true. She knew he thought that and she loved him for it, no matter what else was going on between them.

Harris came out from behind the counter and brought Angie's Chai latte out on the patio to her himself. He smiled and nodded to Tom, who was smoking, and handed Angie a piece of pastry wrapped in a napkin.

"It's our new Starbucks pumpkin loaf," he said after apologizing. "A free sample."

Angie broke a bit off and fed it to Rowena. Harris stood there for a moment, like he was expecting someone to say something.

"Looks like the dog likes it," Tom said finally. Harris seemed relieved. He nodded his head energetically and grinned before stepping back and starting into the store.

"What's with that guy?" Angie asked, sucking the foam from the top of her drink.

"He's got a crush on you."

"Please."

"No, really," Tom smiled. "He's got a huge crush."

"Fuck him," she said. "He gives me the creeps."

"FUCK YOU!" she yelled, turning her head slightly towards the door.

Harris didn't hear her. He thought the whole thing had gone pretty well. The A-Grade Walsh heat strengthened safety glass door had done its job. It was up to five times stronger than annealed glass of the same thickness, and its soundproofing properties made it standard issue at Starbucks stores located at busy intersections all across the country. Harris walked back to the counter smiling. He may have even whistled.

CHAPTER TWENTY-TWO

His love for her was pure to the point of ruthlessness, but he was still a man. The public face and the hidden face. Harris knew she would never love him the way he loved her but it didn't matter. They were fated for each other, and as long as she threw him one once in awhile, he knew they were meant to be together forever.

Love defeats death.

It took him about a week to grow the soul patch under his lower lip, almost as long as it took for the infection from the ear piercing to go away. He'd changed out the stud for a small gold hoop but the hole still bled and pussed. The infected lobe remained red and he squeezed hydrogen peroxide into it as often as it occurred to him. Now he was thinking about some ink. He'd wanted to get a tattoo while he was in the Army but never got around to it. Now he would. Something military, he thought. He shaved but every other day now and took to carrying a tattered paperback copy of Kerouac's *The Subterraneans* he found in a booth in the back pocket of his black jeans.

He was changing his life in many ways for a girl he had no reasonable expectation would ever give him the time of day. It didn't matter. What had his life been anyway? Meaningless and empty. Drinking with a loser like Tony at the Drawing Room? Blowjobs from a future welfare queen like Cookie? His life had been a stupid waste of time.

He had the nightmares he dealt with, but the headaches got worse and worse. This was something different, something new entirely. There was no going back now. He couldn't change what was happening, he could only try and make it come out the way he needed it to.

It was like a battle of good versus evil except that everyone was evil and there was nothing you could do about it except whatever you could to get what you wanted. That was how Angie lived. That was how that asshole Tom Heaton lived. That was how they all lived, all those people who went to the East Hollywood Starbucks, Harris thought. The people he thought for so long were better than him, all those people he was now starting to find out were the same sort of self-important schmucks and losers he could find in far less fashionable sections of Los Angeles. Or anyplace else. They were all bad people, selfish, uncaring and vain.

He'd only put himself in that world so he could get next to her. Now he had to play their game, he thought, play it like nobody they'd ever seen. He felt the headache coming on and reached over for his medicine.

***

Once, at the Washington Square Diner in New York City a long time ago, Tom had come across Al Pacino, alive and in the flesh. The diner was a little, homey place by the early 1990s but forty years earlier it had been a famous lesbian bar called the Pony Stable Inn. In 1967, Andy Warhol chose it as the setting for *Nude Restaurant*, starring Brigid Berlin, Taylor Mead and Viva.

It was a hot summer afternoon and he stopped in for a beer and a hamburger after buying a new pair of boots at one of the shops on Seventh Avenue. A smelly old bum walked in and sat at the counter, asking for a glass of water and the location of the restroom. He was in the process of being thrown out by the restaurant's Greek owner when Pacino's instantly recognizable voice boomed from the back of the room.

"Sir? SIR?..." he caught the owner's attention. *"He's with us, sir. We're going to be shooting a movie here in the neighborhood over the next seven months or so... We'll be in here a lot."* Tom turned to

see the great man, who was sitting in a booth behind him with another guy. *"We're actors, we'll be in costume, if you could just give the gentleman whatever he wants and put it on my bill..."*

The owner shot the homeless guy a nasty look as he handed him a menu. The bum smiled, the few rotting and yellowed teeth remaining in his head shown to great effect. He never looked at Pacino or acknowledged him in any way.

"Thank you, sir. Thanks very much," Pacino said to the owner. *"You know when you're making a movie things can seem kind of crazy..."*

The actor turned back to the other man in the booth and resumed their conversation. Tom grinned and ate his hamburger and drank his Heineken and even though his modest repast -- along with the footwear -- had cost him every last cent he had in the world he felt well satisfied. For a hundred bucks or so he'd gotten a new pair of boots and a private performance by the greatest film actor in the world.

And now, all these years later, he sat in his apartment in the Hollywood Hills overlooking the intersection of Sunset and Hollywood boulevards, his memory prompted by an article he was reading in *Slate* about the various depictions of food in Warhol's art, and he remembered that afternoon. He remembered looking forward to Rachel coming home from work so he could tell her about it. And he remembered how those boots felt when he slid them on, just down the block on a bench in Washington Square Park, and how he took his old boots and put them in the box and the bag and left them on top of a garbage can for somebody else.

One sunny afternoon in Manhattan. Everything was different then and he smiled at the thought of it. New York was long ago and far away now, and Tom thought about putting Pacino into the novel.

***

149

An odd disquiet had settled over Rachel. She wasn't looking forward to going back out to LA, she wasn't looking forward to seeing Tom and she certainly wasn't looking forward to seeing that fucking groupie whore girlfriend of his. She had a dermatologist appointment that morning and then did a little shopping before lunch.

New York no longer seemed like her town. It had stopped being the comfortable place she'd known for the last twenty years. She remembered when they moved uptown, just before Tom filed for divorce from his second wife, Marlene. Everything was perfect then. They took a small front studio at first, the only thing open in the building. Later, a floor-through one bedroom became available and they took that. Finally they moved into the garden apartment, two bedrooms and two baths on the ground floor. They never had any children, never even discussed the possibility as far as she could remember, but they'd been happy. Or so she thought.

She'd gone with him to Alaska to fish for salmon and to Maine to hunt for bear. To Mexico City and the barrios of Cancun and Merida chasing a war he never quite caught up with. What a lot of shit that book was. What a lot of phony heroics. His phony brushes with the famous and famouser, phony bedroom bullshit, nothing but advertisements with which to snag new women and sources of funding, which was all he was about. The phony drunk-ass bastard, she thought.

"Can I get you something to drink, Madame?" the young waiter said as he handed her a menu. Probably some kind of fag, Rachel thought.

"I think I'll have a Bombay and tonic today," she said, looking in her purse for her reading glasses. She had the same thought every day.

Mexican Bloodbath, she thought. The only blood Tom ever saw in Mexico was in the bloody bullring. And how that had sickened her. How she cried. It was like watching little boys torturing a cat. She couldn't look. She closed her eyes and blocked out the sounds of the crowd until all she could hear was the shutter of Tom's old Leica, cycling again and again, preserving the animal's final moments of agony like flies in amber. For sale later to *Corrida!* or one of the other magazines he sank low enough to work for.

He was like an angel of death, floating around the world and taking it with him wherever he went. Living off it, writing about it, taking pictures of it. Dead animals, dead people, dead relationships, dead ideas.

The waiter brought her drink and she ordered a half rack of barbecued ribs with corn bread, macaroni and cheese and sweet potato fries. And another Bombay and Tonic, please. And why not make it a double? Key lime pie for dessert.

In her purse she had a brochure from the Spanish Language School at Guanajuato, where she was thinking about going. She loved Mexico and the Mexicans, happy in the face of disaster, and she liked the food and the music and the economic superiority she had by just being an American there.

She was going to have to get away for a while. That was for sure.

***

"Starbucks. It's perfect," the private detective said. "They go there twice a day. Like clockwork. They bring their dog and Heaton's a smoker so they sit out on the patio."

On the computer screen in front of him, Joey Carson looked at a map of East Hollywood. There it was, next to a bank at the intersection of Hollywood and Sunset and Vermont, set under the watchful gaze of the Griffith Park Observatory in an upscale residential area the tourists were drawn to in the hope of actually seeing some celebrity in his or her own neighborhood.

"You'll love it. It's open to vehicles on three sides and

there's a ton of light," the detective continued.

"And they'll definitely be there?" Carson asked.

"They'll be there. I've been tailing them three weeks and they go every day."

Joey was home now, in Dallas, but he found himself thinking about Manhattan, where he'd just come from, and Los Angeles, where he was going, and he tried to figure out why a smart television guy such as himself was consigned to some goddamn flyover state like Texas when fruitcakes like Tom and Angie and Rachel and even that fucking Melissa Totten got to live the high life and have rock stars for next door neighbors. Here he was, busting his ass, ten, twelve hours a day, six days a week at least, and none of them even appeared to have jobs.

Melissa took the cake. A model? Really? Other than the pictures she had taken for her portfolio, which were all over the internet now, Joey and the private detective had been unable to find anything she'd done. Anything that might have a paycheck associated with it. She was fucking hot though. The braces made him crazy, and if he played his cards right he might just get some of that before it was all over.

For now though, he satisfied himself with her Twitter feed. She posted like fifty times a day.

"My cat scratched me so I killed her," she wrote. *"Hahaha just kidding. I threw her down the stairs. Hahaha. Just kidding. I killed her."*

"I've been in LA for two weeks without a car. This feels worse than whatever is going on in Darfur," she wrote twenty minutes later.

"Put a handful of chocolate covered espresso beans in my pocket and went into the bathroom to cry. Models, am I right?!?" came a few minutes after that.

The way these people worked their Twitter and Facebook accounts made him wonder whether or not they actually had assistants doing it for them. There were so many updates during the course of a day that it seemed to him there wouldn't be time for much else.

"In a coffee shop in LA working on my screenplay about a model who moves to Los Angeles to write her screenplay."

Running into Tom Heaton that night in Pasadena had been the biggest break of her career, and the *Cheaters* episode would be for Melissa what *Gone With the Wind* had been for Vivian Leigh. He'd have her in the last scene, of course, that last scene in the show where the betrayed wife confronts the philandering husband, where all hell breaks loose and emotion is raw.

The critics always said *Cheaters* was too contrived but what the hell wasn't? The Pacquiao-Bradley fight? Obama versus Romney? Please. Everything on TV was contrived, deliberately manufactured to the point where even retards could understand it. It was supposed to be.

There's a good guy, there's a bad guy, there's some issue that brings them into conflict and thirty minutes later a different show comes on. About the ex-wives of professional basketball players or the kids of dead lawyers with cool last names. What a fucking joke.

Did anybody really think that the President of the United States, who was supposed to be the most powerful person in the world, actually got picked by a bunch of middle American nobodies walking into a booth and playing with a touchscreen?

Fuck that. Did anybody really think the President of the United States *even was* the most powerful person in the world?

So Starbucks it was. Starbucks it would be. Joey finished up with the detective and sat back in his chair, putting his boots up on the desk. This could be the big one, he thought. The young starlet and the aging glamour girl, the broken down writer and his vengeful wife, all set against Upper Manhattan and Hollywood and sure to be the biggest episode in a long time. A two-part season premiere that he'd gotten not just twice but three times the budget for.

He had all his bases covered. Airfares, hotel reservations, security, camera crews on both coasts and a hefty chunk of change to the LAPD West Bureau, Hollywood Division. He'd learned long ago that all it took was one prick cop to ruin an entire episode, happening by during the confrontation and thinking that something more sinister than the taping of a bottom feeding reality TV show was going down.

You just never knew, though. There were so many variables.

On the computer screen in front of him, Melissa Totten posted again.

"Wearing my retainer to bed if you know what I mean. (Wearing my retainer to bed.)"

Jesus Christ, he thought. Jesus Christ.

CHAPTER TWENTY-THREE

"Go wash your hands," she said.

He was under the hood of the Cadillac, putting a quart of oil into the crankcase. The morning was beautiful, dry, with a cool breeze blowing big puffy white clouds across the sky.

"I'm doing something," he said, stating the obvious. "Wait."

"Go wash your hands right now."

He looked up.

"Why do you want me to wash my hands?"

"Because I want them clean when you put them all over me."

She stood on the sidewalk in the morning sun wearing a tight ribbed white tank top that came down just far enough to cover her ass, the soles of her bare feet burning on the concrete and her bare white legs luminous in the light. Rowena jumped and played around her feet. He set the red plastic oil bottle down on the engine block and wiped his hands on the brown paper bag the oil had come in. A Lucky dangled from his lips.

"Lose the cigarette," she said and he dropped it into the street and stepped on it.

She gave him the eye from behind a pair of vintage green Lucite framed reading glasses. Her black hair was piled high on her head and fell around her face. Her perfect alabaster hands held a single white gardenia out in front of her.

"Get your greasy paws off me," she said when he got to her.

Up in the darkened bedroom he couldn't even wait for her to get wet. He was on her and in her and he heard her talking and the bed hitting against the wall. He couldn't understand what she was saying and he didn't care. He closed his eyes and kept moving. She dug her nails into his back. She began to moan and lifted her legs high in the air behind him. She wasn't even horny but it felt so good. They began to sweat, their bellies sticking together and peeling away as Tom rose and fell against her. He kissed her on the lips and her tongue darted in and out of his mouth. She was everything to him and he heaved into her one last time then came apart at the seams. She was so fucking beautiful.

When she went to the bathroom afterward, she saw her own blood mixing with his cum on the inside of her thigh. It hurt and it turned her on.

***

They were at the kitchen counter eating out of a cut watermelon with big tablespoons. His robe was black silk and hers was soft red flannel. Her green eyes were dreamy and fixed on him. She didn't know what he was going to say next. He wasn't happy. It was six thirty in the morning and the kitchen light was on. Red watermelon juice dripped from the corner of his mouth.

"You can't go out to dinner with Heather without I have to look at a picture of you with your arm around some scumbag the next morning on the internet?"

Heather was a world-class rock and roll photographer and Angie's best friend in Los Angeles. They often went out together and Heather always had her camera.

"I got my picture taken. So what? It's not like I went out on a date with him."

"I know that. You know that. But that scumbag's on the phone right now telling somebody what a great piece of ass you were."

"Why? *Because that's what you would do?*"

"Everybody who fucking sees that thinks you went out with him."

"I don't care what people think."

"Yeah? Well I care what people think and if people think my girlfriend's getting banged by every scumbag in Laurel Canyon it doesn't fucking look good. For me."

"You don't understand," she said. "It doesn't matter who's standing next to me in the pictures. All that matters is if I look good. Whoever's standing next to me is a prop. The only reason there's other people is so I'm not alone. Posing like some loser."

She always made the weirdest sort of sense.

"The other person doesn't even matter," she said. "Only I matter."

He couldn't argue. At the end of the day even he was a prop, a piece of theatrical property used to further production. To advance her storyline. She was the same for him, he guessed.

She thought for a moment and laughed.

"All you care about is yourself," she said.

He laughed too. She was the most beautiful woman he ever saw. He kissed her and held her tight. She told him she loved him.

***

Tom had come to Hollywood looking for love and fame and fortune, the same things people had been coming to Hollywood to find for a hundred years. He was at the edge of the world, there was no farther to go. He walked through the kitchen, out the back door and into the beautiful afternoon, sundrenched and warm, and he looked at the skyline of the city in the distance. It was the American Dream. Blue-collar kid from upstate New York with money in the bank and living in the Hollywood Hills with a gorgeous actress. It was what everybody in upstate New York and places like it dreamed about.

Yet somehow he felt uneasy. The life he'd meant to leave behind was still with him, still inside of him, and when it came to the surface – the drinking and whoring and the demons, the hard demeanor of someone who'd chosen to live much of his life in dicey and dangerous situations – it all combined now to threaten the new life he'd found. There was a battle going on in his heart and in his head. He could be a loser or a winner. And he didn't know how it was going to work out. Not a fucking clue. He was fairly talented and charming, and he could afford to buy a girl a cup of coffee, but he knew from bitter experience that didn't always get it done.

He stubbed the cigarette out in the big tin Art Deco ashtray Angie had bought him and went back inside. She was at the kitchen sink, rinsing out some cups. He hugged her from behind and kissed her on the back of the neck.

"I love you," he said.

"That's your problem," she replied.

CHAPTER TWENTY-FOUR

Working at Jack in the Box had been a pretty straightforward fast food experience but Starbucks was something else altogether. Everybody thought they were Britney Spears or James Franco. They got mad if they thought their order took too long or if their drink had been made incorrectly.

"Believe me," Harris told Tony. "Nobody can tell whether there's six or seven shots of butterscotch in a butterscotch mocha, it's impossible."

The people on their fucking cell phones, staring at you – or not, you never knew – from behind the darkest glasses on the planet like you were some kind of bug. The baristas themselves were snotty because they all thought they were too good to be working at Starbucks and they were pissed off because their careers as actors or musicians or writers weren't coming along as quickly as they'd planned.

"You never used to talk about your job," Tony said. "Why do you talk about it now?"

"I don't know. I thought it would be… more," Harris said.

"You've got a bunch of pretentious assholes who think that paying five dollars for a cup of coffee makes them rock stars and the people working there knowing they've got to slave away for an hour just to afford that five dollar cup of coffee themselves," Tony said. "It doesn't sound like a happy place."

"It's just this female, man, I just wanted to get close to her," Harris said.

"What?"

For the first time he told Tony about Angie, all of it, about meeting her that night with Cookie and their subsequent brushes, who she was and what she'd done, the way she'd changed his life.

"So you totally changed your life just to be at the Starbucks some chick goes to? Some chick who's not a stripper at Jumbo's Clown Room but told you she was?"

Harris just looked at him.

"Whoa," Tony said before calling down the bar. "Cheyenne, could we get a couple more over here please?"

***

For Melissa Totten, the whole thing was a joke. Still, the dim glow of minor celebrity she had basked in over the days following her Twitter outing of Tom Heaton was fading, and it concerned her.

"*My followers are dropping like its 1848 and everyone is dying of dysentery on the Oregon Trail,*" she wrote. "*I guess if you're going to be miserable though, you might as well be miserable in LA, because at least you'll look cool.*"

But her narcissistic need to post on Twitter and Facebook denied her the ability to even look cool, despite her lithesome figure and schoolgirl smile. It was discouraging. The "Cheaters" taping was next week, but that had been it. Not one other legitimate offer. Yeah, a lot of show business kind of guys had called her and her agent, but it became clear right from the get go that all they were interested in was getting laid. She pandered to them on her Twitter feed.

"*Is it the third or fourth date when you discuss anal? I'm sorry I just blacked out, where am I?!?*"

Even with the taping, the "Cheaters" episode wouldn't air until September so there'd be no press from that. She couldn't even get on that fat ass Chelsea Handler's show. Melissa was already trying to rebrand herself, thinking at first that if she provided insightful commentary on the sort of reality fame she desperately sought for herself, she might be able to catch on

160

with Howard Stern or somebody like that.

"*Should I watch the three-hour Bachelorette finale or kill myself? Wait, did that bachelorette chick have sex with the last two guys before she made her decision? I would've picked the guy with the larger cock.*"

But no matter what she tried, her numbers were plummeting. In desperation, she began to bait low level, former, and in some cases, big-name celebrities. If just one reacted, it would put her back on top, she thought.

"*You guys know I'm actually Shannen Doherty, right?*"

"*Hey Russell Brand: shut the fuck up.*"

"*Is it "you-in" McGregor, "eww-in" McGregor, or 'fuck' you?*"

"*What's on tv? – Casey Anthony probably, I don't know.*"

"*Anyone need a date to the Emmys? I look STRAIGHT UP BITCHIN in a dress.*"

Or;

"*Philip Seymour Hoffman's best role was clearly Dusty in Twister.*"

But it was all for naught. No famous people or quasi-celebrities responded to her taunts. Nobody thought her commentary was interesting and she was discovering that desperation is never sexy. Even at the age of twenty-eight, this final realization was coming to her a bit late, as it does to all beautiful women.

"*...and her ice cream melted because she spent 45 minutes looking for parking in Koreatown.*" – *Excerpt from my suicide note...*" she wrote finally.

They all thought about suicide from time to time. They had to. It was the biggest move a fame whore could make.

In a happy world, Melissa might have wound up with Harris. He could have put his restaurant experience to work starting some upscale though unpretentious hamburger and coffee joint and she could have been the hostess – "former model" being about the best resume qualification there is for a restaurant hostess in Hollywood.

But this isn't a happy world and, aside from the astronomical odds against Melissa and Harris meeting and hitting it off, even if they did, each of them would have thought they were far too good for the other. Melissa was convinced that the only difference between her and Rebecca Romijn was the latter's marriage to John Stamos, while Harris had his heart set on Angie and Angie alone.

Only the most beautiful woman in Hollywood would do.

***

Back at Harris's apartment, Tony was horrified. Pictures of Angie covered every inch of open wall space. Her eyes, her mouth, her ass, her tits were everywhere. In color and black and white. She was very beautiful, there was no question about that, and she photographed really well. But there was something else, something he couldn't put his finger on. A certain feeling she projected through the camera lens, not through her eyes or any other body part, but with her entire being that said you could have a chance with her and that, if you got her, it would be the best you ever had.

Harris brought out a couple bottles of Ratwater Brotherhood Ale and poured a couple shots of Black Velvet.

"She's fifteen years older than you, dog," Tony said. "I mean she fucking slept with Warren Beatty for fuck sake."

"Just a number, man."

"What? Did you really just say that? Because, seriously man, she's about old enough to be your mother."

"Don't you fucking talk about her like that," Harris flashed.

"Are you kidding?"

"Fuck you Tony."

"No, fuck her," Tony said. "Because everybody else in Hollywood has."

Harris was across the room in an instant and punched Tony so hard in the side of the head that his glasses flew across the room. Tony dropped and hit the carpeted floor with a thud.

"Jesus, Harris," he said, shaking his head and propping himself up on an elbow.

Harris was standing over him, his arms cocked to strike another blow. There was rage in his eyes and he was breathing through his nose.

"You shouldn't have said that, Tony," he huffed. "You shouldn't have said that."

"I guess not," Tony said, rubbing the side of his head.

"You shouldn't have said that," Harris said again.

From the carpet, Tony reached over to the coffee table for his drink.

"Where's my glasses?" he said, downing the shot.

***

"So I met this great lady last night, older lady, and she was walking her dog down Vermont and she stopped in front of a large painting that had been thrown in the trash," Tom said. "It was a horrible seascape, the kind people with no taste buy to put over their couches at those 'Starving Artist' events, and whoever threw it away leaned it up against a light pole upside down.

"'That picture's upside down," the lady told her dog, and it was like how I talk to Rowena and I smiled and said I didn't think it would be greatly improved by turning it right side up. She laughed and I asked her the dog's name and she said Shirley Jones. Her last name was Jones and she named the dog Shirley and when she brought it home from the vet one time she noticed they had typed 'Shirley Jones' on the card.

"She said she had three cats at home, Sheba, Sheri and Shelly, and she had a thing for alliteration so she named the dog Shirley. I asked her if she was a writer and she said no and asked why and I told her

163

she was the first person I'd met in Los Angeles who could use the world 'alliteration' in a sentence correctly."

Tom laughed. Angie stared at him blankly.

"Turned out she was an English teacher," he added with a laugh, but to no avail.

***

The prettiest people can be the ugliest, Harris thought, looking across the counter at his customer. She was a young woman, twenty or twenty-two, with long blonde hair in corn rows wearing a tight yellow wife- beater, Daisy Dukes and a pair of Candie's peep-toe platforms that made her four inches taller than she actually was. Hollywood was full of girls like her. Cunts who thought they were all that. Like all about money and status, right? Fucking whores. She was screaming about something, he couldn't hear. When the headache began, creeping up from the back of his neck through the base of his skull and finally splitting the crown, the tinnitus got so loud, the ringing in his ears deafening. And they all deserved to die, didn't they? All the phonies and whores and pimps and queers and addicts who came in all day and night and ordered their Very Berry Hibiscus or Americanos or Cinnamon Dolce Lattes or Espresso Con Pannas and thinking that music or movies or writing or any other fucking kind of "art" justified the sorts of sick, superficial lives they led...

When he came to, Harris was sitting in the little back office. Jimmy was trying to get him to drink some water from a cup.

CHAPTER TWENTY-FIVE

She was on the phone in the other room. He lay on the bed partly covered by one of the Egyptian cotton bed sheets she'd stolen from some hotel they stayed at and he stared up at the ceiling fan. She knew exactly what to do, what he liked, and she was good at it. The best he ever had.

"*Look at Marianne Faithfull,*" she said. "*I mean, just because you used to be hot once doesn't mean you're hot any more, baby...*"

"*Yeah, right... I love her too, but...*"

"*I mean, she was waddling down the red carpet like there was a buffet table at the end of it...*"

"Saigon," he laughed aloud. "Shit. I'm still only in Saigon."

A black candle and some incense burned on the nightstand. She appeared in the doorway naked, her perfect lithe body like a young girl's, posing, head cocked to one side for the phone, her other hand holding out the warm wet washcloth she'd use to mop up.

Because he wasn't in Saigon, he was in Hollywood.

"*Please... She looks like a housewife from Cleveland,*" Angie said. "*She looks worse than some of Tom's ex-wives...*"

Over on Vermont Avenue Megan Fox and Crispin Glover were having coffee on the sidewalk outside La Palermo with January Jones and talking about the possibility of the *Valley of the Dolls* remake finally getting the green light with Megan as Ann, January as Jennifer and Crispin as Tony Polar. It had already been rumored that LiLo had taken the role of the crazy Neely O'Hara.

Jacqueline Susann sold thirty million copies of that book, making her one of the greatest writers in history by Hollywood standards. January said she was excited to be working with Gus Van Sant and Crispin said how cool it was that they all lived in the same neighborhood. Megan kind of cringed.

Angie took the warm wet washcloth and wiped the cum off of Tom's belly. He felt like he was doing porno. She shook her ass. In apartments and cafes all around Hollywood people were fucking or fighting or getting high or talking about their latest project. It was like a dream world. It wouldn't be real, except for that it was.

"But is Tony's madness real?" Crispin asked. *"What does 'antic' mean, exactly?"*

Audiences and critics had debated the question forever. Now Tom closed his eyes as Angie put the warm cloth to his cock, squeezing the last juice up and out from the bottom to the top and eliminating the question of staining the sheets.

He groaned. It felt so good. The warm breeze blew in the window and the shades fluttered. He wanted to have sex again immediately. And he wanted to smoke some more medical marijuana. He wanted everything and nothing.

"Oh come on," Angie said into the telephone. *"It's not like she didn't know what she was getting into…"*

Tom smiled. He thought of all the places he'd ever been. And now he was here.

She was back in the bathroom getting dressed. He got up and put on his robe and went out to get a cigarette from the pack on his desk. He checked his Facebook status. Jackie DeShannon friended him, he saw.

*** *

And then they were fighting again. On the telephone. She called him a little after lunch. He'd eaten steak and eggs at the Desert Rose with Rowena. It was a beautiful Sunday afternoon in Los Angeles, the palm fronds moving in the breeze and the haze downtown. Not a cloud in the sky.

166

***

The list of offenses for which he might be excommunicated kept growing longer and longer.

"Here's your horoscope today on Yahoo," he said, trying to change the subject. "'You have come to your opinions through your own life experiences, and you have every right to stand firmly behind them. However, you also have to realize that other people have come to their conclusions through their own legitimate ways -- you can't disqualify an opinion just because it doesn't match yours. So don't be too dogmatic in your beliefs. If you close your mind, you will inevitably shut out some people who could enrich your life in ways you don't yet understand.'"

"Fuck you, Tom," Angie said. "I changed my sign. Out with the old. Bye bye..."

"You be needin' a stop sign..." he said. "Proceedin' wit caution."

He heard her laugh a little.

"That's better."

"Go back to where you came from and that sweet troll of a pig wife you married and leave me the fuck alone," she said. "There is no excuse for why I let you worm your way into my life. Stupidity on my part."

"I love you too."

"I can't stand the lying drinking womanizing bad temper neediness... You have no one to blame for this but yourself. Now go complain to one of those other poor excuses for women you've been with."

"I'm not drinking and I have not been with anybody. I... Angelique..."

"You got lucky when you added my name to the list," she said. "Now I only wish I could take my name off!"

Her voice choked.

"Baby, this isn't why you called," he said, but she'd already hung up.

She was wearing a white Bob Marley T-shirt that was much too big for her and black sweats, lying on the green velvet Art Deco sofa she had in her living room. The room had hardwood floors and a fireplace and in front of the sofa there was a black marble coffee table. She wished she'd never met him. She began to cry.

Everybody gets their heart broken once in awhile, he figured. Now it was his turn again. It was like there was a big hole inside him he couldn't fill. He wished he was dead.

He'd read an article that morning about the lost pages of the Aleppo Codex. To this day those 200 Holy pages remain the object of intense searches conducted around the globe by priests, private detectives, shadowy dealers of antiquities and the Mossad – Israel's CIA.

Tom's quest was more solitary, and the thing he was looking for would matter to him alone.

***

From the main office roof at the Disney Prospect Studios, the former Vitagraph Studios, Melissa Totten looked down into the back parking lot of a small apartment building on the next street over. There was a man carrying a basket of clothes from a lesser building attached to the garage. He was barefoot and wearing his fake Ray Ban sunglasses with an open red shirt and black jeans. She watched him cross the hot concrete parking lot to a green wooden stairway, which he used to get up to his apartment. Using the same famous iPhone she'd used that night in Pasadena, she snapped a picture.

"Wow," she said. "That's him! This is where he lives...?"

Tom never noticed Melissa or saw Joey Carson and the

"Cheaters" camera crew. They were always shooting something over there anyway. Back up in his apartment, he began folding the laundry.

Carson had arrived the day before and called a friend at Disney about shooting on the roof. They didn't really need any footage like that but he was hot to bang Melissa and, since she was living in Hollywood anyway, he cooked up the shoot as an excuse to spend the extra day with her.

The manufacture of phony saviors is the fundamental concern of Hollywood, its *raison d'etre*. The cemeteries are full of volunteers, from James Dean to Sid Vicious to Marilyn Monroe and Amy Winehouse, Kurt Cobain, Heath Ledger and Anna Nicole Smith. And now Joey had Melissa, that delicious object of desire, contract signed and creative juices all flowing.

He'd have Rachel out there in a couple of days and there'd be plenty of time for business after that.

***

Jimmy sent Harris home and told him to take the next day off. Then he wrote an email to corporate.

"Our Starbucks at Hollywood and Sunset may have a problem," the memo began. *"A recent barista hire may be causing some turmoil, both with members of the team and with our supporters in the community..."*

Work for fucking Starbucks and you've got to learn a whole new language, Jimmy thought. He hated to cause trouble, but Harris just gave him the creeps. He didn't like having him around. Where were the fucking standards, you know? There used to be a certain cache to working at Starbucks. Like even your day job was cool. Now they were letting the hamburger flippers in.

***

When he finished folding the laundry, Tom sat down at his desk to write. For some reason, he'd been thinking of the author Michael Dorris, whom he'd interviewed for The Irish Echo in 1997 following publication of Dorris's Irish novel, *Cloud Chamber*.

They had the author ensconced at the Sherry-Netherland and when Tom got there Dorris offered him a drink, ordering up a double vodka tonic from room service.

"I'd love to join you but I have a reading later," he said, getting himself a cup of coffee.

They chatted for an hour or so, Dorris talking about his book and his writing, Tom asking the same questions he asked most every author he interviewed for the *Echo* and, all in all, it was a pleasant April afternoon in Manhattan.

Because he was leaving for Boston in the morning on business, Tom banged the feature article out when he got home and emailed it into the office. Although he was their chief literary correspondent at the time, Tom only rarely went into the office.

He rode the train to Boston the next morning, took care of his business in the evening and, the next morning cabbed it back to the Boston South Station to catch the train home. He stopped at a newsstand to get some coffee and picked up a copy of the *New York Post* to read while he waited.

The editors had devoted the two-page center spread to the news. Tom couldn't believe his eyes.

"SUICIDE ENDING FOR CELEBRATED NOVELIST!" the headline screamed.

Sometime after the interview, a few hours maybe, Dorris had driven himself up to Concord, New Hampshire, checked into the Brick Tower Motor Inn there, downed most of a bottle of barbiturates and a quart of vodka then took a plastic bag and put it over his head, using a rubber band to create an airtight seal around his throat. Turned out he was going through a bitter divorce and his wife, the author Louise Erdich, was claiming Dorris had sexually abused one of their adopted daughters. The charge was about to come out in some court papers so he killed himself.

Tom went to a phone booth and called into the office.

"What the fuck did you say to that guy?" his editor asked.

Why Tom thought of Dorris now, he didn't know. But it bothered him that he did.

CHAPTER TWENTY-SIX

The whole thing had hit Rachel hard, of course. Tom's desertion was the worst thing that had happened to her in her whole life. It crushed her. She began taking mood elevators and sleeping pills to deal with it, and her drinking had become even worse. She spurned calls from her family and friends and sat by herself in the apartment watching television or going out to restaurants and eating alone. She kept gaining weight and didn't care.

She had loved him more than anything. She loved him more than God. *Why hath thou forsaken me?*

What the fuck is a 50-year-old middle class former newspaper editor supposed to do? There wasn't any warning. It's not like she had any time to fix herself up. After awhile, she began to get rid of the furniture, piece by piece. A few of the antiques she sold back to the stores she brought them from, but most of the stuff she just had the doorman and the super come up and carry down to the curb. Pretty soon there was nothing left in the apartment except for her bed and dresser. She watched television shows and movies on her Kindle. What was the point? Nobody was coming over to sit in those chairs anyway. The only people who had ever come were Tom's friends.

She'd derailed her own career to follow him, typing, editing, mailing, cooking and cleaning, and fucking, at first. Things hadn't been right in the bedroom for a long time, years, but Tom didn't talk about it and she didn't think it was a big deal. They had so much else between them, she thought, books and travel and their adventures. She asked him one time where they were going next and he said Montreal. "What are you going to kill in Montreal?" she asked and he laughed. They were going to see a hockey game, he said. And now he was gone and her life was shit and she missed him so fucking hard.

She moved about the apartment in the dark, empty room to empty room, crying and carrying one of the kittens she'd rescued. Why? Why did he have to leave? She put up with a lot from him over the years, a whole hell of a fucking lot. And now he was out in Hollywood with that cunt bitch. It was humiliating.

The phone rang and she saw it was Joey Carson. She didn't pick up. Her flight was at four the next afternoon out of LaGuardia. She wondered whether she was making a mistake, whether embarrassing Tom and his whore on television for the entertainment of strangers was a good idea.

It didn't matter. It would happen whether it was a good idea or not. That was how these things were. Once everything was set in motion, there was no turning back. She wanted to scratch that bitch's eyes out. She wanted to hurt her, tear her hair out by the roots. Angie Roscelli could've had any guy she wanted, why did she have to pick her husband?

Rachel tripped on some loose carpeting and fell down. The frightened kitten bolted, scratching Rachel's arm and drawing blood. There was a knock on the door and she got up and went to answer it. She turned on a light. It was the doorman.

"Mrs. Heaton," he said, not really sure whether he was getting through to her. "The neighbors are complaining about the cat odor. Would you like me to come in and change the litter boxes for you?"

"Fuck you," she said, closing the door.

***

Manhattan he could take or leave, but Joey Carson loved LA. It reminded him of Ft. Worth. He'd upgraded his rental and was driving a white Mustang convertible with a black top and three hundred horses under the hood. He wore a loose, short sleeved button down shirt that reminded you of a Jimmy Buffet record and Levi 501s and low rent Dan Post cowboy boots. Texas and all that.

Melissa sat in the passenger seat, strung out on some kind of psychotropic Joey had no idea of and wearing a black string bikini underneath a white T shirt and green pumps with four-inch heels. She was the bomb.

"If another male actor tells me good luck at an audition I'm punching him in the dick," she said, apropos of nothing.

"*Don't come on my face and tell me it's raining. Wait, that's not right*," she tweeted.

Joey reached over and put his hand on her bare thigh. Both of them were wearing cheap, oversized black plastic sunglasses they thought made them look like movie stars. Most people in the flyover states would think they kind of did. It was late in the afternoon, and he was taking her to the Power House, a dive he knew on Highland near Hollywood Boulevard. It wasn't the kind of place anyone from LA would even go to, but if you were from Texas or Michigan or Ohio it kind of seemed like a joint you might go to back home. They were staying up the street from there at the Best Western.

Any luck at all and they'd be staying in the same room, he thought, but once they got inside the low dark bar Melissa struck up a conversation with a tall skinny bass player who was currently living crashing on a friend's couch somewhere in the Valley. The guy walked her back to the hotel, where she let him fuck her all night long. Joey had another drink and left pissed off.

***

Tom's agent Hank recognized early on that, more and more, writers were being celebrated for their personal

174

biographies or their online followings rather than for their work on the printed page. Google and Amazon were running the show now and Facebook, Twitter, Tumblr, YouTube and any number of literary networking sites and blogs served to gas up the machine.

Page views, Facebook likes and Amazon affiliate fees were the new coin of the realm. Literary criticism had died once "being nice" took hold as a primary objective. Tom didn't know it, but he was the sort of writer born to live in this brave new world. Hank knew it, and he knew that a war chasing, drunk, mobbed up, womanizing author like Tom was an exotic and grotesque hothouse flower crashing through a world where most books were written by instructors at various colleges and universities. People didn't like books anymore, but they could be made to like authors. It was all about fame, notoriety and, of course, that pungent whiff of what they called "authenticity."

When Tom, without speaking to anyone, decided to leave his wife and his life in New York and go to Hollywood and the arms of someone like Angie, Hank could have kissed him. It was exactly the right move. He'd used up New York, and Rachel could edit a manuscript but certainly wasn't the type who attracted attention.

He had brought his client along carefully, the only real worry now being that Tom would drop dead before the plan paid off.

And even that wouldn't be so bad. Hank had thought about it. He'd still have his fingers in Tom's pie post mortem, and for a writer like Tom, dying could very well be a breakthrough career move. The numbers spoke for themselves. That Totten woman's Twitter ambush was responsible for selling twenty-five hundred copies of *Mexican Bloodbath* in two weeks. Who could say how much business the "Cheaters" program scandal was going to generate?

Tom's novel, a *roman a clef* about Hollywood and celebrity, was substantially complete, and the storm gathering around the author could pay big dividends down the road.

Hank and Joey Carson went way back, to their college days in Florida when they both worked as carnival barkers to put themselves through school. They'd scammed their way from Tallahassee to Key West and had a ball. It would be good to see him again.

He punched Angie's number in on his speed dial.

"Hello?"

"Angie, this is Hank Donato."

"Hi Hank!"

"Angie, the reason I'm calling is, quite honestly, to see where things stand with you and Tom right now. I'm getting a sense, from both of your Facebook posts, that things haven't been good."

"He's still a drunk and a liar, if that's what you mean," she said. "He doesn't give a shit about himself so why should I? That I wasted so much of my time on someone like him... I must have forgotten who he really was for a second, that he's a man who lives his life with no respect for himself or others."

"Well, that's what I wanted to talk to you about, Angie. I know he's hard to deal with sometimes, but Tom's been a new man since he got out there with you."

"He's still too much like the old one."

"What if I came out there? What if we both sat him down and just talked some sense to him?"

"I've tried, Hank. Believe me I've tried."

"I know you have Angie, but maybe if we were both there, you know, the girl he's in love with and his business partner?"

"I don't know."

"I'm going to be out there on Thursday. Do you think you could get him to...? Hey, I know. He sent me a short story to read last week, a chapter from the new book, about a guy who works at Starbucks..."

The details didn't take long. Angie would get Tom to take her to Starbucks at 10 o'clock on Thursday morning. "Let's take Rowena for a walk," she'd say. When they got there, Hank would show up and they could confront him, like an intervention.

Angie loved the idea. Drama was her specialty. Somewhere outside, a car radio played "Witchy Woman" by the Eagles and she bopped a little dance across the living room floor.

CHAPTER TWENTY-SEVEN

He got up, put on some coffee and let Rowena out into the courtyard before sitting down in front of his computer. There were three emails waiting, all from Rachel. He looked at the time. It would be a quarter to eight in New York, which meant she'd been up all night. It had been almost nine months since he left her, nine months in which she'd been unable to accept what had happened. She was seeing a shrink and taking all kinds of pills but it didn't seem to be doing any good. She was drinking like a fish. Why didn't she go to Europe like she'd been talking about before he left? Anything would be better than sitting around their old apartment obsessing about what a bastard he was. He lit a cigarette and opened the first one up.

"*I was just looking at online photos of your girlfriend,*" Rachel wrote. "*Not by any stretch of the imagination is she beautiful. Attractive, yes, about as attractive as that whore Sharon who used to pour your drinks at Mickey's. I must be insane to put up with this bullshit. I have restrained myself but if that spiteful little cunt ever calls me again I'll destroy her. Does she have a tee shirt for most vicious whore on the Sunset Strip? The fact that you can even stand her makes you reprehensible.*

"*I don't want to talk to you, your family, anyone you know. You are all fucking shit. Pay me my money. You fucking fraud. You chide and bully me. What's so bad about me?*

"*Twenty years ago I could only afford to give you $2 a day, along with the free room and board and cigarettes and running a hotel for all your friends and buying all the Midnight Dragon Ale you could guzzle and projectile spew. Now you blame me for everything. Everything. The fucking weather. And I used to go and see your grandmother with you. I insisted we always see her, and bring her goodies, take her out. I sent her presents on every holiday.*

"*You suck. Your book sucks. Thanks for utterly destroying my* *life. You were so fair, you really tried to be fair. That's how you got $120 grand to spend and I got $25,000. Pay me my fucking money.*

"Nothing that happens to you can be worse than you deserve. I supported you for seven years working at the Post. I gave up my career for you. You spent your paycheck at Mickey's and the Press Box. You're fucking pathetic. Send me my fucking money and my future payments and leave me alone forever.

"Now you've lost the beer gut, how about getting dentures that don't make you look like an inbred retard, and that fit. Jesus Christ, kissing you was like gulping scum off a pond.

"Something is wrong with you mentally, part of your illness. You dumb fuck I hope you die soon along with that filthy gash that gave you herpes. I'm not going to tolerate this. Don't ever call me, don't ever contact me again."

The blue, early morning light was beautiful and Rowena trotted back up the stairs and Tom let her in the screen door. "My good girl!" he said, giving her a treat and filling her bowl with water from a bottle of Pellegrino he took out of the refrigerator.

He never had herpes and neither did Angie as far as he knew, but Rachel's second post was somewhat more conciliatory. It was early September and even at that time of the morning it was hot. He came back to the desk with his coffee and sat down and read what she'd written.

"Tommy, do you think anyone will ever love me again? Because I am so torn up. Please respond and tell me the truth. I want you to know I am trying my very best. Oh, it's been hard. But things have happened the way they happened. I love you and hope you are okay. I will do anything to help you. I am sorry too for all the misunderstandings and craziness.

"I want to get married again and I can't see myself going through years of loneliness waiting. It is killing me right now. I want to have some surgery because clearly you just realized you could get a prettier girl. Around here men never look at me or speak to me... Love, Rachel"

Christ, he thought. She'd written that just forty five minutes after the first one. That was the thing about alcoholism. As the loftier registers of insight, memory, judgment, concentration and understanding become dulled and then lost, personality changes can occur as well as uncontrolled mood swings. Emotional outbursts can become frequent.

And it was always those quiet, mousy lushes who were the worst. All sweetness and light until they got that crazy look in their eye just before plunging the knife in your back. He opened the third email, written a half hour after the second. It was crazy. She was driving on all sides of the road.

"Lucky lucky lucky you. Today's your lucky day! This is the day I will kill myself."

She'd threatened it before. A lot of times over all the years, and over a lot of things. She never did it, but he never got used to it. He knew she was capable. She hurt herself all the time.

Now Angie was hating on him and Rachel was hating on him.

Still making women miserable on both coasts, he thought.

Beneath him just then, the chair shook and beneath that the floor. The building's foundation shook and the earth into which it was set shook too. Out on the street, all manner of car alarms were rocked into action, wailing and screaming and whooping in the still morning air. Rowena trotted over and looked up at him, then jumped up into his lap and licked him on the face. Tom petted her and waited. It was just a tremor.

"Rowena's the bestest girl," he said finally.

***

Over in Los Feliz, Angie watched *CNN*, where an overheated black man was telling about the earthquake. Angie had lived in Los Angeles all her life and once just about had a house come down around her ears but like many Angelinos, she

180

was somewhat fatalistic about the tremors.

"Seismologists say a mild earthquake widely felt throughout Southern California was centered near Yorba Linda, about forty miles southeast of downtown Los Angeles," the man said. "The quake measured 4.4 on the Richter Scale. Fire Department spokesman Matt Spence says firefighters rolled out of stations citywide and surveyed 470 square miles. No infrastructure or other damage was found, and no injuries were reported. Actually Bill, Matt Spence, the Fire Department spokesman, said this wasn't much of a quake at all."

She was still wearing the big Bob Marley T shirt and hadn't bathed or even gone out much since talking to Rachel. Her beautiful green eyes were sad and red with tears. He was a fucking piece of shit but she loved him and if he didn't come to her she would go to him. Fucking bastard.

Rachel called drunk two days before and told Angie that Tom had been in contact with her the whole time he'd been in Los Angeles. She said he told her he wasn't at all attracted to her, that he just used her to get out of the marriage and gather material for a book he was writing about Hollywood.

"He said you gave him herpes," Rachel told her. "He said you were stupid."

Angie knew that if she asked Tom about it he would deny it, but how could she believe him now? How could she ever believe anything he said ever again? What Rachel said hurt her. She felt sick to her stomach. But she missed him so bad. She wanted him touching her, holding her, taking care of her and saying that everything would be all right. Her resolve ebbed by the hour.

It was like she was frozen by indecision. It had been so long maybe she'd forgotten but, if this was what love felt like, you could fucking well have it. Goddamn him.

She took another tissue from the box and dabbed her perfect nose, then drank from a bottle of unsweetened Snapple peach tea. On TV they were going on and on about the earthquake, which had been no big deal. She glanced down at the phone. Why didn't he call?

***

Harris thought the earthquake was a hallucination brought on by his headache and took another handful of pills. It was the same sort of rumble in the ground you feel when the artillery is firing the big 155 mm shells over your position toward the enemy in front of you. Like sitting on the ground by the tracks when a big freight train comes roaring by.

But then the chick on *FOX* said it had been an earthquake and Harris hoped it was the little one before the big one. He hoped against hope. He wanted nothing more than to see the city devastated, a death toll in the tens of thousands and, as far as he was concerned, the epicenter could be that corner where Sunset intersects with Hollywood and Vermont. He imagined the earth moving under the feet of those phony fucking Silver Lake hipsters, looks of sheer panic and horror in their eyes. The blood that would flow when the roof caved in.

He'd seen death. Up close and personal. He'd caused death too, as simply and deliberately as another person might use a remote to change the television channel. That kid came out of nowhere. Harris spun around and fired at the sound. The soccer ball the kid had been chasing kept rolling as the kid crumpled dead. It was ruled an accident and it was an accident, but he had done it, snuffed out a young boy child's life, and the revulsion and guilt overwhelmed him.

His head was fucking splitting and he drank the Black Velvet straight from the bottle. His eyes felt like they were going to pop out of his head. Sweat dripped from his face and the T-shirt and blue hospital scrubs he wore to bed were soaked through. He thought he could hear the cracking along the sutures that held the bones of his skull together. He wanted to cry out but didn't.

He'd spent the night cramming the tiny, bottleneck 7.62x25 mm cartridges he'd bought into the magazine designed to accept them. It got harder and harder to depress the spring with every round loaded, and by the time he'd filled it his fingers were bloody from the sheet metal edges of the magazine lips. They were all full now, thirty-two rounds in each of the five sticks. Enough to kill one hundred and sixty people, theoretically at least.

There was one thing he knew. He knew it like he knew his own name. When the big one came, he would be ready. Ready, willing and able.

***

When Rachel finally passed out, her bags were packed and set over by the door. She wore a green Anne Klein suit she'd paid retail for and a pair of strapped brown brogues with two-inch heels she ordered through Amazon. She'd had it. Her hatred for Tom and her hatred for Angie overwhelmed anything that might have once been decent about her, and the seething rage she felt consumed her.

She would destroy them both. She would have her revenge.

***

Over at the Highland Avenue Best Western, Joey Carson slept his alcohol fueled sleep drooling on the pillow while, in another room on a different floor, Melissa Totten was being banged into the headboard moaning and sweating by the tall skinny bass player who lived crashing on a friend's couch somewhere in the Valley. It had been hours since they all left the Power House and Melissa's eyes were rolling up in her

183

head, cocaine and vodka and all that. None of them noticed the earthquake. They wouldn't have noticed it if it had killed them.

***

Tom couldn't go back and erase the things he'd done, the women he'd fucked, the booze and the dope and everything else. If he could have he would have, in a heartbeat, and he tried, but that's not the way things work. He was who he was and there was nothing he could do about it. Going forward maybe, but there was already too much blood under the bridge.

God fucking America. Didn't he love her.... It had taken him a half a century to find her and now that he had it seemed sometimes like everything in the universe conspired to take her away. And maybe that would be the best thing. She didn't deserve his shit. She hadn't done anything to deserve it.

She wouldn't answer his calls but she messaged him on Facebook. *"Let's talk... Starbucks at 10 a.m. tomorrow?"*

He thought it was odd that he couldn't recall her ever mentioning a specific time like that before. It wasn't in her nature. He wrote back and told her he'd be there. What else was he going to do?

The afternoon was hot and dry and heat came in through the open windows as though they were pizza oven doors. He tried to stay perfectly still but it was no use.

***

Mambo Green Mamba was a *voudon* witch he knew in Paris. She began studying the Kabbalah as a child growing up Jewish in Martinique. The story of how he knew her was complicated and long, but she was a friend of James Williamson's and when the phone rang, Tom somehow knew it was her.

"Mon cher," he said.

"Baruch ata!" she replied in a voice brought low by absinthe. "Blessed His Name and don't ever try to escape from your way, which is to be loving Angelique and being loved by her. Only then will the Sephiroth tree grow straight again!"

"Mambo, how do you even know about this?" Tom asked, shaking his head and thinking of the tree with its branches and leaves at the bottom and the roots at the top.

"I look at the Facebook also..." she said.

He laughed and lit a cigarette. Like any professional writer, he was always looking to distract himself from the solipsistic detention home that was his life.

"You're too late, I think. She told me to go away."

"The one you love can't help loving you, Tommy!" Mambo said. "You are the Cat People, searching for each other since the beginning of time."

"You should tell her."

"I do not have to. Angelique knows. Mon cher, if she was going to leave you she would be gone by now I think. *Non, on ne l'oublie pas, ce chéri!*"

"*Vous êtes un bon ami,*" he stumbled. "*Et ce que vous avez eu jusqu'à?*"

His French must have reminded her she wasn't speaking to someone who spoke French because she switched quickly back to English to answer.

"Oh, thinking of Africa again and again," she said. "The Mambo is changing skin now and it is painful. Afraid of not retrieving a correct skin now."

But always the talk returned to Angie.

"I know she's in love with me, Mambo, but it seems as though the world plots to keep us apart," he said. "Sometimes I think I might just as well be down in old Mexico again, or back in New York for that matter, miles and hours away."

"Would you like it as still water? I doubt it," she laughed.

"You prefer it as a sour posh Irish whiskey!"

He laughed.

"How do you know everything?" he asked.

***

"And that, Harris my man, is the big lie, the one taught to us by our parents and our teachers, the one peddled by the media," Tony said. "A whopper cooked up by Thomas Jefferson himself. All men are created equal. Bullshit! Equal my ass! Some are better looking, or smarter or more talented or have richer parents. Some are born in the United States and others are born in Uganda. Some guys are just lucky."

"I used to think like you, but not anymore," Harris said.

"C'mon man. You can't realistically think you've got a chance with her. She's been married four times and, except for the swimming pool guy, each one was more famous than the last."

"That's just the world she lives in. Those are the guys she meets."

"So you think you've got the same shot as this Tom Heaton? With his books and his money and his rock star cred?"

"He doesn't have the money you think he does," Harris trumped. "I ran a credit check."

"What?"

"He makes a lot of money but he spends more than he makes. A lot more. He's got less than twenty grand in the bank."

"And how much do you have?"

"That's not the point. The point is she married the swimming pool guy."

"Not for long. He fucked it up somehow. Somehow like he wasn't a rock star like the guy she dumped him for after... How long was it?"

"Eleven months but..."

"But nothing. These people stick with their own kind. If she doesn't end up with Heaton it'll be someone like him, only richer and more famous. Not some overage, overweight coffee boy making minimum wage at fucking Starbucks."

"You think that's what I am?"

"That is what you are. It's what you've chosen to be. It's what you do for a living."

Harris couldn't even be angry. He was blank and empty. In all his life, he had never tried to do anything good. And now that he had, he'd failed. He knew it, Tony knew it, Jimmy his manager knew it and Angie and Tom Heaton probably knew it too. He really was a loser. A loser who was never comfortable in his own skin, who'd found success at Jack in the Box then threw it all away for some woman who wouldn't even give him the time of day. Now the things he had were gone and the thing he'd given them up for was laughing at him.

His listless grey eyes fixed their thousand-yard stare into their reflections looking back at him from the dirty glass of the mirror behind the bar.

"I would fucking kill you, you know?" he said to Tony.

"You need to just chill out dude," Tony said.

***

Angie cried and cried. She hadn't been in love for many years and only just now realized why that was so. It was horrible. She hated the way she felt. The way he talked over her. The way he got angry and snapped. She hated his drinking and his past and that cold look he got in his own green eyes when he told her to get the fuck out of his house.

But as much as she hated it -- hated him sometimes -- when he wasn't around she felt empty and alone, even when she was in a roomful of people. She'd force herself not to call him and then break down and dial his number. Her weakness made her feel bad about herself and if he didn't answer she flew into a rage, leaving message after message telling him he was the scum of the earth.

It was hopeless.

CHAPTER TWENTY-EIGHT

The next morning Rachel got on the plane at JFK. She was hungover so she drank on the plane. It was a seven-hour flight. Angie sat at her vanity and primped. She'd never met Hank in person before. Hank was supposed to be flying out of LaGuardia but actually wasn't coming at all, and Joey and Melissa were already in Hollywood. Tom had a headache and felt kind of nauseous but he wanted to win Angie back and he got out of the shower and combed his hair and put on the silk hand printed Burma Bibas shirt, the black silk Bill Blass suit and the alligator Lucchese cowboy boots. With the fake Wayfarers, the whole thing looked kind of put together.

***

Harris gulped down a handful of pills. Even a whiff of coffee now brought a sick headache on. He'd purchased a couple of logo shirts from the Starbucks Gear website and now he became ill every time he put one on. His financial condition was becoming desperate. He could barely get out of bed. When he did, he vomited then took more pills.

What was happening to him? His life before hadn't been great but at least he could pay his rent. Now he'd thrown it all away to pursue a woman who couldn't have cared less about him if he'd been a dog. In fact, she probably would have liked him better if he had been a dog. No, for sure she would have.

Woof woof.

He was sweating profusely as he walked down to the car. Sweat ran down his nearly shaved head and into his eyes and it burned like hell. In his right hand he carried the hard shell case that people would have thought contained a guitar had he been walking down Hollywood or Sunset. He popped the trunk and carefully laid it inside.

***

Angie was happy. Hank had sold the option for *Mexican Bloodbath* to UTA for twenty five thousand dollars, he said. After his cut, that would be more than twenty thousand in Tom's pocket. And he was a guy who knew how to buy a girl a cup of coffee.

If he would just go get some help, step into the light, he would be the perfect boyfriend. Or husband maybe.

***

"I used to be into the light, but then everybody started getting into it," Tom told Rowena as he put on her leash and walked down to the Cadillac. She liked going for rides. It had been nine months since he fled New York for Los Angeles, nine months of paradise, nine months of perdition.

He was feeling good. The novel was almost done now and it pleased him.

He turned the car on and goddamn it if Joe Walsh and the Eagles weren't playing "Hotel California." He wouldn't be able to get that out of his head all day.

***

Joey looked horrified as Rachel got off the plane at Burbank. She could hardly walk. Fuck. It was two hours before the fucking confrontation. All he could do was get her to the hotel and try sobering her up. Back at the hotel he fed her a bottle of Ipecac syrup and when she was done throwing up he forced her to drink a bottle of water. She threw up again and

190

then he gave her another bottle and a handful of aspirin and caffeine pills.

He kept her away from Melissa lest the mayhem start too soon. He'd take Rachel himself in the production van and send Melissa on ahead in a limo. He felt a strange excitement, anticipation and anxiety that quickened his heart and was, for a guy like him, better than sex.

***

When Tom got to Starbucks he saw Angie talking with Kiefer Sutherland, the tall, thin blonde girl who had been with him at Il Capriccio still standing off a respectable distance.

"C'mon girl," he said, and Rowena hopped out of the passenger seat to the pavement.

He walked across the parking lot smoking a Lucky and knowing how lucky he was. He slid his arm around Angie's waist and kissed her on the top of the head.

"Hey Kiefer," he said.

"Hi Tom. Angie was just telling me you sold the option for *Mexican Bloodbath*. Congratulations," he smiled.

"What?"

Kiefer looked at Angie.

"Did I say something I shouldn't have?"

"Don't be silly," she said. "Isn't it wonderful, Tom?"

"Wait," Tom said. "You know my book was optioned and Kiefer knows my book was optioned and I don't know my book was fucking optioned?"

"Nice seeing you again, Tom. Give me a call sometime Angie," Sutherland said, backing away.

"Hank called me," Angie said. "He's worried about you, Tom. He'll be meeting us here."

"What?"

"Just take a table. I'll get you some coffee."

Angie disappeared into the store.

Jesus Christ, Tom thought. Everybody in Hollywood knows what's going on except me. He sat down and dug the pack of Lucky Strikes from his pants pocket and lit one. Rowena jumped up on his lap with her tail wagging.

***

From a van nearby, a private detective watched as Angie came back out, handed the coffee to Tom and sat down to wait for her Chai latte.

Damn, she was hot. Like every other man who saw her, Angie cast her spell over the detective. It was a powerful spell, even at that distance. And she didn't even have to do anything other than be Angie.

He looked at his watch and called Carson to make sure everything would be going down at the appointed time. The two cameramen and two security guys who sat in the van with him were quiet.

***

Hank sat in his New York office as Joey told him about the detective's report. Tom and Angie were at ground zero, with Melissa and Rachel on the way. The crews were already in place and a big surprise was hovering nearby, Joey said. Everything was going along smoothly.

It was perfect. This ought to be good for five thousand copies in a day or two probably, he thought. Tom's whole backlist. It might cause his old friend some embarrassment, it might even cause a nervous breakdown. But for a short while, a couple of days at least, Tom would become the most famous author in the United States. And that was worth any sacrifice.

***

192

When Joey realized Rachel was as sober as she was going to get, he hustled her into the van and had the stylist work on her there. They sped away from the Best Western and headed east on Hollywood Boulevard.

Harris pulled into the parking lot and got out of his car. He walked around to the back and started to open the trunk when he saw it all coming down. Just as Angie was coming back to the table with her drink, approaching Heaton and that mutt Chihuahua at their table, two women, one who had been in a limousine and the other in a windowless white van on the other side of the lot charged toward them screaming and shaking their fists, followed by some big guys in blue SECURITY T-shirts and other guys with television cameras on their shoulders. Angie screamed back at the women and as Heaton tried to hold her back, she dropped her Chai latte splashing on the pavement and got off a roundhouse right that knocked the younger and smaller of the two screaming women to the ground.

Harris forgot all about what he was doing and ran reflexively toward the melee.

***

When the helicopter swept low over the roof of the store, Kiefer Sutherland put his hand on the top of his head and said to the tall, thin blonde woman who accompanied him, "What the fuck, I can't even leave the house anymore."

He was set to star in a new police procedural and thought the cameras and the helicopter were there for him. Fucking TMZ, he thought. Fucking Harvey Levin. He was worried about his hair.

"C'mon. Let's get inside," he said to the woman, grabbing her by the elbow and heading into the store.

Up in the chopper, Joey tried to direct the chaos that was

taking place down in the parking lot over a radio.

"Is that Kiefer Sutherland getting up from the table directly behind the subjects? Over..." he said. "Repeat is that Kiefer Sutherland down there? Because if it is Kiefer Sutherland somebody better get him in the goddamn shot!"

***

A fat sweaty guy in a cheap suit stuck a microphone in Tom's face.

"You've got a wife and a live-in mistress and you try to pick up young lingerie models in hotel bars," the guy said. "How can you even live with yourself?"

Tom decked him and turned to see Angie struggling with some other guy.

"Let me go, you fucking asshole!" she yelled.

"C'mon Angie," Harris said. "I'll get you out of here."

"Get your fucking hands off me and mind your own goddamn business," she said, kicking and screaming.

"She's with me," Tom said when he got to them. He took Angie by the shoulder.

"Did you get Sutherland? Repeat. Did you get Sutherland?" Joey asked again and again. The chopper's rotor threw a cloud of dust and gravel up in the parking lot.

Tom was trying to get Rowena's leash untangled from around his ankles and didn't see Rachel, his wife, coming up on the blind side.

"You fucking groupie home wrecker," she cried, sinking her claws into Angie's black mane. Angie bent over double but then straightened up and kneed her antagonist in the groin. Rachel released her death grip on Angie's hair and threw up on the sidewalk.

"Your home was already wrecked, you goddamn fat cow," Angie said over her shoulder as Tom led her away. "And I told

194

you I'd fucking hurt you, I told you..."

***

Once it was all over, Angie dragged Tom into the store, where she demanded to see the manager.

"Look," she said, fixing her hair. "This asshole has been harassing me since he started working here. He said I looked like a stripper, he lets people smoke out on the dining patio and just now he actually put his hands on me. He grabbed me. I'll sue this goddamn place."

"What's your side of this?" Jimmy the manager asked Harris.

"I was just trying to help..."

"Did you put your hands on her?"

"I thought she was going to get hurt."

Jimmy suspended Harris on the spot.

"You won't have to see him again," he told Angie. "If he's not let go outright they'll transfer him to another store."

"Well I want to know what that store is," Angie said. "So I can make sure I never go there."

Harris drove back to Glendale in a daze, forgetting what he'd put in the trunk, forgetting what he'd intended to do when he went into work that morning. His head was splitting.

"You should have fucking seen it," Joey said to Hank. "We got Angie taking on Melissa and Rachel both, Tom punching out a photographer, we even got a cameo by Kiefer Sutherland, which was totally by accident!"

"I wish I had been there," Hank said, blowing out a cloud of cigar smoke. "And the show's airing in September?"

"September 13 and 14," Joey said. "Season premier and it's solid gold."

Hank loved it when a plan came together. His secretary had already fielded a call from a reporter wanting to know whether

Tom Heaton had actually assaulted a Hollywood paparazzi. There would be press straight through, police involvement, raw footage leaks via YouTube… The possibilities were endless.

"This is fantastic," Hank said. "We are going to make the fucking *Times* list."

***

On the way home, Tom accused Angie of colluding with Hank to ambush him.

"Where the hell was he? You said he was going to be there," he said angrily. "Did the book really get optioned or did you make that up too?"

"Fuck you, Tom."

The conversation quickly degenerated once they got back to the apartment.

"YOU WERE NEVER ANY GOOD IN BED!" she screamed.

"Fuck you. You said that was the best you ever had. A million times better than Mark Knopfler, you said."

"I LIED!!!!! YOU COULDN'T EVEN GET IT UP WHEN I MET YOU AND THE ONLY REASON YOU CAN NOW IS BECAUSE I'M SO GOOD IN BED!"

"Get out of here," he told her. "Just go away."

"I'll go and I'll never come back," she spat, heading for the nearest closet. "You're nothing but a wolf in sheep's clothing."

All his closets were filled with Angie's clothes. She began pulling down handfuls of hangers and throwing them on the bed. Then she stormed out of the bedroom and past him towards the kitchen.

"And I'm taking all the dishes. Because they're mine! I bought them!" she told him, coming back out with a roll of Glad tall kitchen bags.

Back in the bedroom she stuffed the Chanel and the Dolce & Gabbana and the Anna Sui and the Vivienne Westwood into the garbage bags side by side.

"Why don't you go back to that fat pig of a wife?" she said walking out the door with the garbage bags. He knew she'd come back for the dishes so didn't bother trying to stop her. *"You two deserve each other!"*

The screen door banged behind her.

***

He told her his love for her was so strong that if she felt leaving him would make her life better, he wouldn't argue and he wouldn't bother her after she was gone. He lied. She should go and never look back.

"It was worth it, baby," he said. "I've had the most beautiful girl in Hollywood for the last nine months and I can die a happy man."

She looked as though he'd slapped her. Her dreamy green eyes teared up.

"Oh my god, don't say that, Tom." She hugged him around the waist and buried her face in his chest. "Don't ever leave me…"

"You know I could never let you go," he said, hugging her back. "The love of my life."

Later they lay intertwined like a couple of snakes, holding each other tight. All night long. They didn't even do anything. They just held on.

CHAPTER TWENTY-NINE

Harris pulled into the parking lot at their usual time, that whore and her lush and their precious little mutt. They treated that fucking dog better than they treated other people, he thought. The ringing in his ears was overwhelming. His headache had hurt so bad for so many hours that it now felt normal. He opened the trunk and flipped the latches on the hard shell case. He slammed a magazine into the receiver then put the others into his back pockets before walking deliberately toward the store. When he got inside, he raised the weapon. He heard a girl scream and that was all.

***

MacBook Pros and iPhones smashed as they were dropped by wannabe actors and musicians and models. The world of performance art lost some exciting young prospects. The days of workshopping scripts ended for at least one aspiring screenwriter when a 7.62mm slug tore through Jimmy the Starbucks manager's right eye and buried itself deep in his brain.

***

"You just smelled smoke and you just kept hearing it, you just heard bam bam bam, non-stop. Shots just kept going, kept going, kept going. I'm with coworkers and we're on the floor praying to God we don't get shot, and the gunshots continue on and on, and when the sound finally stopped, we started to get up and people were just bleeding."

"I started seeing flashes and there was screaming, I just saw blood and people yelling and a quick glimpse of the guy. I was pushed out. There was chaos, we started running. Everybody thought it was like fireworks or something like that, and then you just see people dropping and the gunshots are constant. I heard at least twenty to thirty shots within that minute or two. It went on and on and then after we didn't hear anything, we finally got up and there was people bleeding, there was people obviously may have been actually dead or something, and we just ran up out of there, there was chaos everywhere."

"He walked in so casually, like he knew what he was doing. I heard two pops. Everyone was distracted. That was when the panic and the chaos started. He started shooting, and everyone ducked and started screaming. He looked like he was ready to go into battle. It was like he was walking around and having fun. Emotionless..."

"There was this girl. She just had this horrible look in her eyes. We made eye contact and I could tell she was not all right. I had to go. I was going to get shot."

"People were running everywhere, running on top of me, like kicking me, jumping over me. And there were bodies on the ground. I froze up. I was scared. I honestly thought I was going to die."

199

"The image in our heads is stuck in there. I still have my cup right here and honestly, I'm never going to forget this night at all. Because it was the first time I saw something that was real. Like a real-life nightmare that was there, not dreaming of."

***

The carnage was horrific. When it was over, Harris and twenty-two other people lay dead and dying on the sustainable ceramic flooring Starbucks was justly famous for. Another dozen had been shot and wounded before Harris put the muzzle of the weapon up underneath his chin and pulled the trigger, ending his headaches for good.

It was the biggest mass murder in the history of California, bigger even than the San Ysidro McDonald's Massacre down in San Diego all the way back in 1984. Harris had outdone himself.

The East Hollywood Massacre, they'd call it later, and it was all because of one man's obsession with unattainable splendor. A reach that exceeded his grasp. Politicians would use the incident in arguing for more gun control.

***

It was a gorgeous summer morning and Tom and Angie left before it got too hot. Down in the courtyard she stopped him and kissed him softly on the lips.

"Why you kissing on me today?"

"Because I'm your girlfriend," she said.

Her fair skin always looked magical in the sunlight. When he was with her it was like he was on vacation.

She pretended not to smell the scotch on his breath just like she pretended not to know he had a fifth of Johnny Walker Black disguised in a Listerine bottle he kept in the bathroom medicine cabinet. She just didn't want to fight any more. She loved him and that was all.

He drove down Talmadge and turned right on Prospect and that's when they first heard the sirens. They got louder and louder as he drove past Hillhurst towards Vermont, and Rowena barked at the police cars, fire trucks and ambulances rolling through intersections with their red and white lights flashing.

"What the fuck?"

From where the cop stopped them down the block, Tom and Angie saw the aftermath of the tragedy. The dead and the wounded being put into a coroner's meat wagon or any of a half dozen ambulances. Cops in bulletproof vests carrying machine guns. The A-Grade Walsh heat strengthened safety glass windows shattered and shot out, television cameras and satellite trucks everywhere, reporters with microphones, screaming survivors, the whole nine yards.

"I don't know what happened, but they ain't serving no coffee in there this morning," Tom said.

"God fucking America!" Angie yelled. "I need my fucking tea!"

Tom threw the Caddy in reverse and backed up to the corner then turned down the side street.

"That's all right, baby," he said, making the right onto Melbourne. "Don't worry about it. We can just go over to the Starbucks on Los Feliz."

They were made for each other. He put his hand on her leg. She smiled and threw her beautiful white arms around his deeply tanned neck and kissed him on the ear.

"Oh daddy, that's why I love you so," she said.

About the Author

Mike Hudson was born in Cleveland, Ohio. He published his first journalism and short stories in 1977, at the same time as the Pagans, the seminal punk rock band he fronted, began recording and touring.

His writing has appeared in publications as diverse as *Radar*, the *Irish Echo*, *Hustler*, *Master Detective*, *Field & Stream* and *Paraphilia*.

Hudson currently lives with his five dogs in a ramshackle house off Topanga Canyon near Malibu.

Fame Whore is his sixth book.